Where The Turnpike Starts

By HARRIETT H. CARR

Miss Carr spent most of her growing-up years in the state of Michigan. We can therefore look to her book **WHERE THE TURNPIKE STARTS** for some expression of her feeling for her homeland as she tells the story of young Anne Rogers against a background of the turbulent years of Michigan's struggle for statehood.

In reading this exciting book, we are always first concerned with Anne's adjustment to her new environment in the Michigan wilderness, but early in the story Anne's imagination and loyalty are fired by the boy Governor, Stevens Thompson Mason, and with her, her father and her friends, we are caught up by the exciting events which lead finally to Michigan's being taken into the Union on January 26, 1837.

AGAINST THE WIND

BY HARRIETT H. CARR

WHERE THE TURNPIKE STARTS
AGAINST THE WIND

AGAINST THE WIND

By Harriett H. Carr

THE MACMILLAN COMPANY
New York

To George H. Fern

Adversity is the prosperity of the great.
Kites rise against, not with the wind.

(From "Something to Live By"—Dorothea Kopplin)

1. *The Decision*

STEADILY, persistently, the immigrant train whistled its way northward from Chicago toward Minneapolis. Five coaches, three baggage cars, and a small red caboose trailed behind engine and coal car.

"W-o-o-o-o-o!"

Dan Osborne was used to it now. He was familiar with the smoke that blotted out the snow-covered March landscape and the cinders that seeped through the cracks around the windows. He had even become accustomed to the cramped space between the red plush seats where there was little enough room for his long, husky legs and to Pa's irritable grumbling about it too. Little Grace and Eddie in the seat behind had plenty of room, of course. Six and eight years old they were, and their feet didn't even touch the floor. As for Mom, she never stayed in one place long enough to get cramped. Up and down the coach she went, visiting with all the women and getting acquainted with everyone.

"W-o-o-o-o-o-o! W-o-o-o! W-o-o-o!"

Dan strummed softly on Slim's old guitar. If he could only play like Slim! Slim had learned so easily and twanged the strings so briskly! But Slim was two years older than Dan; nineteen he'd be by now. Pa had been willing to teach Slim, too. After Slim ran away, most a year ago, Pa hadn't seemed to want anything to do with the guitar.

"Oh, Susannah, don't you cry for me," Dan hummed to himself. That was an old immigrant song. Melancholy sounding the way Dan played it. Pa said the '49ers sang it as they trekked off to California in the gold rush days. Well, this was 1900 and the North Dakota land boom was on instead of a gold rush, but the song was as fitting as any that came to Dan's idling mind.

"Oh-h-h! D-a-n." It was a terrifying, unhuman sound. Pa! Could that be Pa? Dan turned to his father in surprise. One side of Pa's face was twisted strangely and he was pushing and shoving at his left hand that lay limp in his lap. As Dan stared in bewilderment, his father kept trying to talk, but only choking, unintelligible sounds came from his oddly-changed lips.

"Pa!" Dan gasped. "What's the matter? Are you sick?"

But Pa could not answer and the look in his eyes was frightening.

Slowly Dan's wits came back to him. Something was awfully wrong, but he mustn't show that he knew it. He mustn't frighten the kids, who were quiet now, drawing pictures to amuse themselves.

"You just sit still while I get Mom," Dan said reassuringly. "She'll know what to do. Likely there's a doctor on the train, too."

But would Mom know what to do this time? Dan didn't dare to face the question.

At the rear of the coach Dan spied his mother, talking with another woman. Carefully he stepped over his father's feet and got into the aisle, then hurried clumsily toward her, swaying with the jerking train.

"Mom, Pa's took sick. Bad," Dan blurted out and his shaking voice sounded strange even to himself. "You'd better come quick."

For an instant Mom stared at him, as though she couldn't believe her ears. Then she was on her feet, pushing past him into the aisle, her new friend close behind her.

"Mom, do you suppose there's a doctor on the train?" Dan asked as he followed them.

"I don't know, Dan," she answered. "Go find the conductor. He's probably in the smoker."

"I didn't tell the kids, Mom," Dan called after her. He didn't know whether his voice carried above the noise of the grinding wheels or not. But it wouldn't matter much anyway. The kids would know in a minute or two, at most.

Reeling with the coaches, Dan made his way to the smoker. Babies and rag dolls and suitcases blocked the aisles. Throughout the train there was the odor of engine smoke and hard-boiled eggs and sandwiches. Unpleasant odors, of a sudden. But these were the same coaches, the same smells that had been with him since he left his home in Cincinnati. Exciting it had been, when they took the train for North Dakota and the free farm Pa and Mom had been talking about ever since Gramps died.

Dan looked for the conductor's blue cap and brass buttons. He was in the smoker as Mom had guessed, sitting in the first seat with tickets and slips of paper spread out in the empty space beside him.

"Conductor, is there a doctor on the train?" Dan asked, interrupting his sorting and counting.

"A doctor?" the conductor repeated, pulling off his glasses for a better look at Dan. "What's the trouble, Red?"

Dan liked his nick-name. People sounded as though they liked him when they called him "Red," and usually they grinned at the bush of unruly dark red hair that never would stay parted.

"My Pa was taken sick awfully sudden," Dan explained. "Charles Osborne's his name. He's up in the second coach ahead."

The conductor wrinkled his thin nose and put his glasses back on. He didn't say anything as he gathered his papers together and slipped a rubber band around them, but he nodded to himself and kept wrinkling his nose.

"Now don't you get upset, son," he finally said. "There's a doctor here somewheres. Bright young feller, he appeared like. Jest you wait and I'll find him."

Dan watched the shiny, blue-serge suit as the conductor swayed down the aisle, peering at the passengers.

"He must be up ahead," he said when he returned alone. "Come on along. I'll find him."

Back through the train they went until they reached the coach where the Osborne family was riding. It was clear at once that someone had already found the doctor. He was bending low, his stethoscope at Pa's heart, and Dan could see little of him except the top of his dark, thickly curled hair.

"Your heart's fine. Steady as my own," Dan heard the doctor say as the conductor pushed people back out of the aisles and made way for Dan. Then the physician spied the conductor.

"We need snow to pack on this man's head, conductor," the doctor said. "Is there some way we could get snow?"

He didn't wait for an answer, but removed Pa's coat and pushed up the sleeve of his good arm. From his satchel he took a wide band with tubes attached and wound it around Pa's arm. Men and women on either side watched, and glanced at each other knowingly. Mom, standing in the aisle, held Eddie and Grace back in their seats.

"Come on, Red," the conductor said. "We can't do much here."

At the front of the train the conductor stepped to the coal car and signalled to the fireman, while Dan held breathlessly to the open door. The rushing air stung his cheeks and tears smarted his eyes as the train slowed to a stop.

"Take that bucket there, Red," the conductor called. "Hop down and be quick about it."

Dan clambered down the iron ladder to the solid, snow-covered ground. After hours of ceaseless motion on the train, the earth seemed swaying and reeling too.

"Pack it in solid," the conductor ordered. "We can't stop again until we get to the next station. But there's more snow than anything else from here on to the Pacific coast."

Dan packed the snow down solidly. Then, back in the train, he watched intently as the physician scooped handfulls into a towel, twisted the heavy cotton deftly, and placed the snow pack on Pa's head.

"I'll hold it," Dan offered. "I'm his son. I'm Dan Osborne."

"I'm Dr. Johnson," the physician said, then turning to the women: "Which one is the wife?"

Mom answered and followed as he motioned her to the back of the coach.

"The doctor said it's a real light stroke," one of the women assured Dan as he sat on the arm of the seat, holding the snow cap in place on Pa's head. "I don't reckon he'll be laid up long. The Doc gave him some pills to quiet him. You can count on me to help, if need be. I'm Mrs. Martin."

Dan thanked her. Pa was indeed much quieter. He didn't try to talk, his eyes were closed and he was breathing easily. But his face looked unnatural and his left hand still lay limp in his lap.

Gradually people stopped peering and settled back into their seats. Dan tried to think reasonably about what had happened. There had been no warning. Pa had been grumbling a lot lately and that wasn't like him, but he hadn't said he felt bad. This was all unreal. Like something he'd heard about that happened to somebody else. Dan wasn't sure he understood the meaning of this sickness that had come upon Pa.

When Mom came back Dan was re-packing the snow in the towel, twisting it tightly as he had seen the doctor do it. Mom motioned him to follow her to the empty seat where she had been sitting, and Mrs. Martin took his place beside Pa. But Mom couldn't talk when she got there. She laid one hand on Dan's arm and swallowed once or twice, and looked out the window at the darkening landscape.

"Is he awful sick?" Dan finally asked. "Isn't it best that I know?"

"Yes, you've got to know," Mom said and her voice, always deep and husky, was scarcely audible. Dan had never seen his mother like this before. Her new purple wool dress, tucked so fine and fitting tight about her large, full body, shook with the beating of her heart. All dressed up she was for this trip, the first trip any of the Osbornes had ever taken. She had put the front of her straight, grey hair up on curlers each night so it would fluff out above her high forehead. And she was wearing her garnet ear-rings and big cameo breast pin. Dan stared at the pin, avoiding her eyes.

"Tell me, Mom," he urged.

She took a deep breath. "Dr. Johnson said if he doesn't have another stroke by morning, he'll surely live," she said at last. "But he'll never be strong again. He'll likely never be able to farm."

"Not be able to farm!" Dan repeated. "Mom, what are we going to do?"

"It's what we've got to decide," she said. "By the time we get to Minneapolis. Dr. Johnson said he'd get a wheel chair for Pa in Minneapolis, if we go on."

"A wheel chair? You mean he can't walk? Ever?"

"Not for six months. Maybe a year," Mom explained.

Dan wiped the perspiration from his forehead with the back of his hand.

"Not on your good pants!" Mom cautioned quickly. "Use your handkerchief."

Dan fumbled and found the handkerchief. His stiff, white collar was tight and uncomfortable now, and his blue wool store suit scratched wherever it touched him.

"Mom, what are you going to do?" Dan asked again.

"Whatever I do, I can't do it alone," Mom said slowly. "I've got to depend on you, Dan. So you've got to help decide."

Dan caught his breath at the suddenness of it. Never before in his life had Mom put anything up to him. She decided, or Pa, or even Slim. He was about to say he'd do as she said, of course. That was always the easiest way, and likely the best, too. But something stopped him now. That wasn't what

–7–

Mom wanted him to say, this time. He thought he understood. Pa . . . Slim . . . She had depended on them in the past. More than she showed, likely enough. She couldn't look to either of them now. He was next in line.

"If we turn back at Minneapolis, what's there to go back to?" Dan asked. "Pa couldn't get his job back at the drug store. Not if he can't walk."

"We've got to count Pa out, Dan," Mom answered. "We've got to figure on taking care of him, not him taking care of us."

"How could we do it, back in Cincinnati?" Dan asked. "You could nurse again, and sew like you've always done. But what could I do that would amount to anything? You know how it was with Slim. How little he could earn."

"We still have the money," Mom whispered. "Back home we could start some little business. A boarding and rooming house, or the likes of that."

Involuntarily Dan shuddered. Down by the depot it would have to be. On the wrong side of the tracks again. And forever! That was what they wanted to get away from.

"If Pa's no worse when we get to Minneapolis, could we still go on and file on the land?" Dan asked.

Mom nodded.

"Dr. Johnson says he'll help us. He's going through to Minot too. He says all Pa'll have to do is sign his name and he can do that if his right arm's still good. Pray God it will be."

For a few minutes Dan watched the telephone poles and snow-covered hills slide past the window. A farm of their own! That was what they all had wanted. Some place where Eddie and Grace could play . . . A horse that would be his . . . A buggy so Mom could drive to visit the neighbors in style . . . Dan had never been on a farm but Pa and Mom had both been brought up in the country. He'd heard them talking about it ever since he could remember.

"Maybe we could start some other business back home," Mom suggested, interrupting his thoughts. "Something more for a man, that you could carry on."

"Gosh, Mom, I don't know anything about any business," Dan answered. "What would it be?"

The conductor stuck his head into the coach then.

"Twenty minute stop for supper at the next station!" he called. "Twenty minute stop!"

People clambered to their feet and put on their wraps. It would be drafty in the station restaurant and downright cold in the corners farthest from the stove.

"Doc tells me he thinks your man'll pull through all right," the conductor said stopping beside Mom. "I don't reckon he'll want any supper though."

"Nor us either," Mom answered, "but I guess we'd best eat. Get the kids, Dan, and my coat. See if Mrs. Martin will stay with Pa for a few minutes longer."

Dan was conscious of people staring at them as they sat together at one of the oil-cloth covered tables. The story was spreading through the immigrant train. Men and women stopped to speak to Mom.

"If I kin do anythin' . . ."

"You'll need help in Minneapolis, likely . . ."

"My Jake here's husky. He kin help carry your man."

Mom thanked them all.

"Dan's real strong too," she replied to the last offer. "But he'll have to manage the baggage."

She was beginning to sound sure, and like herself again, and Dan took courage. Manage the baggage, he thought. That was right. Pa had seen to it in Chicago, telling each one what to carry, keeping an eye on every satchel, and going to the baggage car to make certain their trunks and crates were all right. Dan knew what he had to do. He'd find out where they had to go.

Dan took Mom's elbow when they got back to the train and gave her an awkward lift up the steps. That was what Pa always did when there were people around. He'd not thought to do it when they got off the train.

It was dark when they settled themselves back in their seats and the conductor was lighting the lamps. They'd be in Minneapolis in the morning. In the morning they'd have to decide.

In the morning! What was he thinking about? In the morning they'd have to *know*. They'd have to decide tonight.

Dan turned to his mother. She was looking at him and her eyes, green like his own, were questioning. Had she sensed that he'd not realized the decision couldn't wait?

"Mom," Dan said thoughtfully, "of all the things we could do, like a store or a boarding house, or the farm, what do you know the most about?"

"Why, I guess a farm," she replied. "I was raised on a farm. I've read all the literature your Pa got from the Agricultural College in Fargo."

"Well, I don't know nothing about nothing, Mom," Dan said knowing full well that Pa would have corrected his grammar, had he heard it. But Mom ignored the mistake.

"I know what you mean," she said. "I guess you've got to learn from scratch, whatever we do. So what would you choose to do? Then we'll try to reason out whether it's best or not."

It was easy to answer that question. He knew well enough.

—10—

"I'd choose to go on and get the farm," Dan said.

Mom did not answer him at once.

"Farming's awful hard work, Dan," she said at last. "From daylight to dark, it's hard work."

"I'm not afraid of the work, Mom. It's no different now than before, so far as the work goes. It's just that I've got to do it alone, until we can find Slim."

"Don't count on Slim," Mom said quickly. "He's answered none of our letters and he must have got some of them. The ones we sent to Williston weren't ever returned. There's no one to count on but you and me, Dan."

Dan did not contradict her. Mom and Pa both were bitter about Slim, but Dan wasn't. He thought he understood why Slim had run away to North Dakota. Thought he'd find him, too, although that would likely take time. But Mom was right about this. There wasn't anyone to count on now but the two of them.

"All right, Mom," Dan said. "The question is, can we do it alone? Just you and me. I'm ready to try if you are."

There were tears in Mom's eyes and she shook her head slowly, but she reached over and gave his hand a reassuring squeeze as she tried to smile.

2. Owned by "The Interests"

DAN shivered as he stood in line in front of the Land Office in Minot. All day he'd been standing, except when Mom came to relieve him so he could go to the hotel to thaw out and get a bite to eat. It was dusk now and she'd be coming again soon. He'd try to get a little sleep this time, for he'd have to stay in line all night or lose his place. It would be late tomorrow before he got inside the building at the rate the line was moving.

Dan knew the men in front of him and behind him now, and they knew what the doctor had told him to say.

"Just say your father was taken sick on the train, and I've warned it might run into pneumonia," Dr. Johnson had told Dan. "Say he's being kept inside, but your mother or I will bring him to the Land Office to sign the Register's records when the time comes."

Mom had been opposed to the plan at first, holding that it was a sin to tell a lie. But Dr. Johnson explained that it wasn't a lie; just not all of the truth. She'd consented then. No need to tell everybody all of your business. The Lord had seen fit to lay Pa low, and He'd provided for the doctor too, so likely what the doctor said was all part of His plan, she reasoned. If Mom felt it was all right with the Lord, Dan was sure there was no cause for him to question it.

"Your Ma going to relieve you, come supper time?" the boy behind Dan asked. Chris Nelson was his name and Dan liked him fine. Chris was a Norwegian and his folks came from Minnesota. He was just Dan's age.

"Sure, she'll be along soon now," Dan answered. "If your brother Nels comes at the same time we can eat supper together. If you'd like to, that is."

"Nels will come, that I know," Chris replied. "He never fails. I was thinking, though. I'll ask Pa to do a stretch for your Ma. It don't seem right for her to stand in line after dark."

"I was thinking that too," Dan replied, glancing at the men around him. "I hadn't figured I'd sleep more than an hour or two at most. If your Pa would . . . even for a couple of hours . . ."

"Pa'll do it," Chris assured him. "When we tell him," and he nodded significantly.

It was clear to Dan that Chris shared his fears. Ahead of them a big, sagging man named Ike Sheets had been drinking most of the afternoon. He was waving the bottle freely now.

"If Tom Sheets comes to relieve his old man it might not be so bad," Dan said in a low voice.

"I don't take to Tom much more than I do to his old man," Chris replied. "Only Tom might be sober."

The Nelson boys were blonde and blue-eyed and scrubbed looking and their cheeks ruddied with the cold. Nels was eighteen, a year older than Chris, but Dan had thought him nearer twenty. Big fellows they were and as sturdily built as Dan himself. Beside them Tom Sheets, with his drooping shoulders and slouchy walk, seemed like a scrawny sapling. He entered into the banter and joking freely enough when he took his place in line to relieve his father, but when "Old Man Sheets" was around, Tom had nothing to say.

Dan looked toward the hotel. Frame buildings with false, second-story fronts, lined the street on either side. There was a bank, two or three general stores, a lumber yard, livery stable, blacksmith shop and barber shop, all plainly marked with signs. Some were painted and neat appearing. Toward the edge of town, where rutted, grey hills rolled up above the valley, there were other buildings covered with tar paper and strips of lathe. Already Dan knew some of them were "blind pigs" and gambling halls, although a few were called restaurants.

"For a state that's got a prohibition law—" Dan remarked to Chris, but he left the sentence unfinished as the yelp of a dog drew his attention back to the man in line ahead of him.

"Dirty purp!" Sheets shouted at a little collie puppy that now ran limping and yelping away from him. "That'll larn ye." Ahead of the puppy a rock rolled into the street.

The men in line ignored the incident. It was plain enough that Sheets was not to be reasoned with now.

"Wonder what the poor puppy did to him," Dan said as the dog limped to the shelter of a doorway and sat down to lick his bruised leg.

Chris shook his head. "This line is no place for your Ma, that I know," he replied. "Here comes Nels. You stay in line until I get Pa to relieve you. If your Ma comes before he gets here, send her back to the hotel."

Gladly Dan agreed. He wouldn't be able to sleep a wink with Mom in the line now. But he hesitated at first to tell Nels the story of Ike and the drinking and the pup. Nels wasn't as friendly and talkative as Chris. He looked at Dan inquiringly though as Chris darted off, and Dan had scarcely finished his account of what had happened when Mr. Nelson arrived.

Dan had seen Mr. Nelson early that morning when the family fell into line just behind him. Chris and Nels had been directed to take turns holding the place for their father while he went about the business of getting lumber for a house and barns. Dan remembered him as a tall man with very blue eyes and heavy white eyebrows who had spoken to no one except his sons. He had little to say now, but he laid a friendly hand on Dan's shoulder as he pushed him out of line and stepped into his place.

"Get a good sleep and be easy in your mind," he said and when Dan tried to thank him he waved his hand in a gesture of dismissal.

There was a flurry of snow in the air as Dan started down the street. He paused in the doorway where the puppy was huddled, still licking his leg.

"Poor chap," Dan said leaning over to pet the animal. At first the puppy cringed back, but as Dan stroked its head and spoke again the little dog licked his fingers and whined.

"Poor chap," Dan repeated. "I wonder where you'll sleep tonight."

"Where who'll sleep?"

Dan turned quickly at the question. It was Tom Sheets who spoke. Tom apparently was on his way to relieve his father.

"The purp," Dan replied. "His leg's hurt."

"How'd it get hurt?" Tom asked and his interest seemed genuine.

Dan couldn't tell what had happened. It wasn't Tom's fault. Tom's nose was red with cold and his grey eyes watered a little, and scraggly brown hair stuck out from under his cap. But he was looking at the puppy as though he'd like to pet it too. Likely it was because Dan was there first that he kept his hands in his overcoat pockets.

"What's the matter, purp?" Tom said to the dog.

"Someone threw a rock at him," Dan told Tom evasively.

It seemed to Dan that Tom Sheets knew, right then, who threw the rock. His kindly manner changed and he kicked at the doorstep without reason.

"Maybe someone had a cause to throw a rock at him," he said, suddenly on the defensive.

Dan didn't answer. He leaned over and stroked the dog's honey-colored hair.

"Maybe you'd better watch yourself," Tom said. "Maybe he bit someone."

"I don't think he'll bite me," Dan said. "I'm going to take him up to the hotel and see if I can get him some supper."

Dan took the dog in his arms and carried it to the hotel. Before he got there the animal was licking his face and whining little puppy whines.

A dining room, kitchen, and small parlor that served as an office and lobby were on the first floor of the building. The friendly smell of coffee and frying pork set Dan's mouth watering as he opened the door. Mom was sitting at one of the tables with Grace and Eddie as Dan came in. She was fussing with the sugar bowl, her full lips curled in disgust at the coffee-stained red and white tablecloth.

–16–

"Whatever in the world?" she asked as she looked at Dan. Grace dropped her old rag doll immediately, reaching with eager hands for the dog. Dan told what happened.

"Do you suppose we can keep him?" Dan asked. "We'll need a dog."

"We'll call him Punkin," Eddie announced, scrambling for a chance at the puppy. "He's just the color of punkin pie."

"Punkin!" Grace snorted. "That's no name for a dog. Dogs are named Rover or 'Old Dog Tray' or something like that."

Dan smiled at her. She was Mom, all over again. But Eddie stuck to his point.

"This dog's name is Punkin," he repeated. "And we can keep him, can't we, Mom?"

"If nobody wants him we can keep him," Mom agreed. "You can make a bed for him in our wagon for tonight and we'll see if he's still there in the morning."

"Our wagon?" Dan repeated.

It seemed to Dan that there was considerable pride in Mom's voice as she answered him.

"I bought two wagons, Dan. I figured the time we'd save if we could haul everything out in one trip would be worth the price of a wagon. We've got to get started with the plowing as soon as we've a roof over our heads."

"Your Maw's a right smart business woman, Red," a man at the next table said. "You're Dan, I take it."

Dan nodded.

"I'm Jim Jackson and this is my missus. Maybe we'll be neighbors."

Jim Jackson was a round-faced young man, friendly and cheerful. His dark eyes sparkled and his black hair was slicked back from his smooth forehead. His wife, who didn't look to be more than sixteen or seventeen, was smiling with pride in him.

"Jim's just filed on a quarter section off toward Williston," she said. "Tomorrow he's going to get our horses and plows and things."

"I wisht I was as good a horseman as your Maw, Red," Jim said jovially. "When I first seen her this afternoon she was makin' the horses at the livery stable open their mouths so she could see their teeth, and holdin' up their feet so as to have a look at their hooves, and goin' over 'em as thorough as any man there."

Dan looked at his mother with new admiration.

"How many horses did you buy, Mom?" he asked, trying to appear off-hand about it.

"I guess I was a mite extravagant, Dan," Mom answered. "I got six work horses like Pa said, then I got one other."

"One other?"

"He didn't cost much or I wouldn't have done it," Mom explained. "He's a long-legged black, and he'll never make a plow horse. That's why nobody wanted him. Good plow horses are bringing $150 each, so when I bought six, they threw in this other one for another $35. After I'd dickered a bit, that is. He'll make a good riding horse for you, and a buggy horse later on, I figure."

Dan whistled softly. Mom had certainly done herself proud while he stood in line.

"They otta show you some consideration," Jim Jackson said. "There ain't many comin' out here with the old spondoolicks to lay on the line. Me, I'm already in debt to the Interests up to my eyebrows."

He laughed as he said it, and if the debt held any terror for him he hid it well. Mrs. Jackson looked at him and smiled again. A round little robin she was, and always smiling.

"The crops this fall will take care of that," she said confidently.

Mom changed the trend of the conversation.

"You finish your supper and go get a little sleep," she said. "It was mighty kind of Mr. Nelson to take this stretch for me. I don't want you to waste time talking now."

"As soon as I put Punkin to bed," Dan said, taking food from his own plate to give to the dog, now wagging its tail contentedly as it sat on the floor under the table.

"Let me! Let me!" Eddie begged. "I'll put him to bed."

"That's right," Mom decided. "Eddie and I'll fix the dog a bed. You go upstairs and try to sleep."

But Dan couldn't sleep. He lay on a cot in the room he shared with Eddie and Grace and thought of all the events of the day. Minot, with its two or three unpaved streets crowded with horses and wagons and men in work clothes, was more exciting than Cincinnati ever had been. It was too bad Pa couldn't hear the talk of the men. Everybody eager and enthusiastic. Everybody anxious for the same thing—to get on the land. Poor Pa!

Dan got up and tip-toed cautiously to the adjoining room. Mom had lit the lamp and propped Pa up on his pillows. He was a wiry man and stooped a little, and in his old striped night shirt he looked almost thin. He moved his good right hand in Dan's direction.

Dan had been wondering in his own mind if Pa could hear what was said. If he could understand. Dr. Johnson had said that he could, but Dan wondered.

"Pa, if you aren't asleep . . . I just thought . . ."

Pa motioned Dan to sit on the bed beside him. He moved

his lips, but only a strange sound came, and he waved his hand in a gesture of irritation. It brought a lump to Dan's throat but at the same time he felt a certain relief. For of a surety, Pa could hear and think and understand.

"Don't try to talk, Pa," Dan said. "I'll just tell you what we did today. So you'll know. We got a purp. A fine little collie dog and Eddie named him Punkin. He'll make a good watch dog."

It seemed to Dan that Pa tried to smile. At least his blue eyes were alert and shining. So Dan told him of all the day's happenings and how Mr. Nelson was taking Mom's place in line. But he didn't tell about Ike Sheets and the drinking. That would worry Pa.

Before he was half through Mom came upstairs and sent Dan back to his own room to sleep. He felt better after he'd talked to Pa and went without protest although he knew he'd never sleep a wink . . . And then Mom was shaking him, waking him up to go back into the line.

The banter and joking had ended when Dan stepped into the place Mr. Nelson held for him. Tired, silent men were stomping their feet and beating their arms against their sides to keep warm. Dan looked ahead to Ike Sheets' place. Tom was there now, leaning wearily against one of the buildings and his eyes were closed.

"I'll bet Old Man Sheets'll never show up to relieve Tom this night," Nels whispered to Dan.

"He'll be dead by morning," Dan answered, pleased that Nels seemed to be accepting him.

"So'll you be," Nels replied. "When I come at two o'clock to relieve Chris, I'll bring some coffee, if I can find any."

It was a long, cold wait until two o'clock when Nels returned. Good as his word he brought a pail with coffee, two cups, and doughnuts in a paper bag.

"Old Man Sheets didn't come back," Dan whispered, hoping Nels would sense what was in his mind.

"There's enough," was the reply.

"I hope he'll take it all right," Dan said, remembering the afternoon and Tom's resentment of any reflection cast upon his father.

Nels seemed to understand. "I'll tell him Ma sent it for the two of you."

Dan watched covertly as Nels wakened Tom and offered the food. To his surprise Tom took it, and when Nels urged him to eat more he reached for another doughnut without hesitation. Dan wondered if Tom Sheets had had any supper at all. It wasn't likely his father had given him much money.

Four hour shifts the Nelson boys took. Nels settled down in Chris' place to wait out the next four hours. Dan wondered when Mom would come to relieve him. He hadn't asked her when he came back into line at ten o'clock. He wished he'd brought a blanket as he pulled his overcoat tighter around his legs and huddled on the sidewalk close to a building.

Unfamiliar night noises punctuated the slow hours. The stomping of horses, the bark of a dog, the incessant creaking of a sign overhead as it swayed in the cold wind that swept through the valley. Around him men snored and occasionally cursed as they wakened, stiff with cold. Here and there in the shacks beyond the main street a light burned, but for the most part Minot slept in darkness. Not even a star could be seen in the grey-black sky above.

Dan was wakened by a hand on his shoulder. He sat upright with a start.

"Five hours is long enough," Mr. Nelson was saying. "Go back to bed now, the rest of the night."

Dan got to his feet. Ahead of him Tom Sheets was standing, beating his arms against his sides, shivering with cold.

"His old man's left him here all night," Dan whispered to Mr. Nelson. "Since six o'clock last night." Tired as he was, Dan felt sorry for Tom Sheets.

Mr. Nelson hesitated.

"Your Ma'll not be coming soon," he warned.

"I can stand it," Dan answered.

But when Mr. Nelson offered to relieve him, Tom Sheets turned to Dan in indignation.

"Why can't you mind your own business?" he demanded. "Meddlin' in other people's business, that's what you're always doing. Why don't you let me alone?"

There was grumbling from others in line as Tom's angry voice wakened them. Without a word Mr. Nelson went back to Dan and pushed him silently in the direction of the hotel.

Dan felt sick at heart as he stumbled back along the rutted street. He hoped Mr. Nelson hadn't misunderstood his intentions. He'd made an enemy of Tom Sheets, and no mistake. Well, perhaps he'd never see Tom again. Perhaps their farms would be miles apart. The full length of North Dakota.

Slowly, as the next day passed, Dan moved nearer to the Land Office door. Mom kept an eye on him now and in spite of herself she couldn't hide her nervousness. When Ike Sheets' turn came to go inside and file, she went for Pa.

Suddenly Dan was frightened. Nobody in line had seen Pa. They'd be staring at him, trying to talk to him. Dan's stomach was up in his throat at the thought of it.

Mr. Nelson was behind him in line now, ready to pay his $18 fee and sign the Register's papers. Likely he'd want to talk to Pa. And Chris was sure to. He and Nels were waiting with their father, eager to know where their land would be situated. News had reached the men in line about locations

—22—

that were still available. Way out on the prairie they were, thirty miles or more from Minot. Off south toward Bismarck or west toward Williston. Dan knew where he'd like to locate. If Williston wasn't any bigger than Minot and Slim was there, he'd find him.

Another five minutes, and down the rough street came Mom, pushing the wheel chair before her. Pa was wrapped in blankets that hid him almost completely. His blue wool scarf was tied around his head, holding his cap down securely, and the ends covered his mouth and chin.

Dan's heart began pounding hard. Everybody was staring. No one was saying anything.

Dan stepped out of line to meet his mother as she came along side and he wheeled the chair awkwardly back into his place. After the first sight of Mom, so silent and dignified, the men turned to each other self-consciously or looked the other way, and made conversation about the waiting and the weather. Only Mr. Nelson spoke to Mom and in a quiet voice inquired about Pa's health. No one tried to get Pa to talk. Dan breathed a little easier.

"If they'll only let him alone," Dan thought to himself. "If Ike Sheets doesn't try to talk to him when he comes out."

But Ike did try. He was sober now and pleased with himself as he emerged from the Land Office building.

"Hundred sixty acres right here in my pocket," he announced looking straight at Pa. "Six months from now I can buy it outright for $1.25 an acre. That what you're aiming to do?"

Dan doubted that Ike Sheets had the money to buy the land outright. Most of the homesteaders expected to live on their claims five years, and then prove up by paying another small fee.

—23—

Dan was about to answer for Pa, but Ike didn't wait for an answer to his first question before he asked a second.

"You're Red's old man, ain't you?" he inquired. "I heered you been sick."

Dan looked at his father and held his breath. He wanted to knock Ike Sheets down. But Mom took charge of the situation.

"You'll have to excuse my man," she said. "He's about lost his voice with this sickness. Dan, you wheel Pa inside so he don't catch cold. I'll hold the door open for you."

Dan felt better once the door was closed behind them. There was a measure of security in the bare room and the warmth of the big, round stove, its isinglass windows reflecting the red and blue flare of the burning coal inside. But ahead was the Register, his plots and maps spread out on his table and tacked on the wall behind him. And the Recorder who would take their money. Both men were staring at them.

It was Mom who repeated the doctor's story this time. She looked at the plots and selected the quarter section nearest Minot, off in the Williston direction. Badly as Dan wanted that location he wished he could choose another section when he saw that the land adjoining had just been taken by Ike Sheets.

The papers were made out and the questions asked. Pa's name. His age. Was he head of the family? Was he a natural born citizen? Mom answered them all but each time the Register looked at Pa, expecting him to answer.

"What's the matter?" the man finally asked looking directly at Pa and he sounded suspicious like. "Can't you speak at all?"

Dan burned with indignation. Once more Pa was being humiliated and there was nothing he could do about it. Once more he looked to Mom, but before she could answer Pa's good right hand reached for the paper the Register held.

"Y-e-s."

It was Pa who said it! It wasn't clear and distinct and it didn't sound like Pa at all, but it was a word. An understandable word.

"Pa!" Dan and Mom exclaimed at the same moment.

"Pa, your voice has come back!" Mom almost gasped. There were tears in her eyes and she dug into her pocketbook for her handkerchief.

"Now let him sign the papers so we can get him back to bed at the hotel," she said to the Register, blowing her nose hard.

The Receiver came to their rescue then.

"Can't you see the man's sick?" he asked irritably. "For the love of Mike! Come over here, Red. Sure you understand where your land's situated?"

No one asked any questions as Dan wheeled Pa out of the Land Office and back to the hotel, but there Ike Sheets was waiting.

"Did you get your land?" he asked of Mom, looking furtively at Pa and the wheel chair.

"Yes," Mom replied. "No trouble at all."

"Need any help with your man?" Sheets asked. "I can see he's right bad off. Out here folks has to be neighborly."

It was a generous sounding offer, but Dan was suspicious. Ike Sheets just wanted to find out what was wrong with Pa. But Mom was a match for him.

"Now that's right kind of you," she said. "If the doctor isn't here like he said he'd be, I'd appreciate your help."

Mom must have known the doctor was waiting. He was opening the hotel door at that moment, and with a swift, sure move he slipped his arm around Pa and had him safe inside while Mom was thanking Ike Sheets again.

"That Ike Sheets!" Dan muttered. "He just wanted to find out. He doesn't care anything about Pa. Or anybody else."

"Everybody's going to know about Pa," Mom said quietly. "We couldn't hide it to save us. And we've got to get along with our neighbors, whoever they be. Or try to, at least. Now you run along down to the livery stable and make sure our horses are fed and watered and bedded down good for the night. Just tell the man you've come to see to the Osborne animals."

"The Osborne animals." There was a prosperous sound to it. It made Dan feel good. He forgot about Ike Sheets and his son Tom as he stroked the smooth sides and broad rumps of the big bays that the hired hand at the livery stable led him to. Best of all was the tall, lean black that nuzzled its nose against Dan's arm.

"You're mine, boy," Dan whispered to the animal, running his hand along the sleek, long neck. "You're mine and you're a prince of a horse. Prince. That's your name. Hear me, Prince?"

Oh, it was a good feeling! Punkin and Prince and a quarter section of land! By the flickering light of a lantern hung against the barn wall, Dan cleaned out the stalls, carried in great pitchforks of clean straw, filled the mangers with fresh-smelling hay. Maybe the hired man should have been doing the work. Dan didn't care. These were the Osborne animals!

It was dark when Dan left the livery stable and a cold wind sent snow swirling through the air. Stinging, icy flakes knifed through his clothing and filled earth and sky, all but obliterating buildings across the street. His back against the livery stable door, Dan looked about him. He could see the outlines of the railway station dimly. A train must be coming in, for people were hurrying in that direction.

Then Dan gasped aloud.

Slim! It was . . . it was Slim! There was no mistaking the tall, thin figure, the way he held his head forward, the left leg that bowed out a little at the knee. He was coming toward Dan, hurrying in the dark, snow-filled night to the station.

"Slim!" Dan called. "Oh, Slim!"

Slim Osborne stood still and rigid as a church spire at the sound of his name.

"Dan! What are you doing here?"

There was surprise in his voice. Surprise and anxiety and alarm.

"We're all here, Slim," Dan told him. "Pa and Mom and all of us. We've got a farm. Oh, I'm so glad . . ."

"Glad!" Slim interrupted him. "Oh, what fools!"

Slim's words were sickening, his tone frightening. Beneath his cap, pulled low over his face against the storm, his brown eyes were hard and worried looking. His little, dark moustache outlined a straight, unsmiling upper lip. Dan had seen him like this before. Just before he ran away. This couldn't be! This wasn't the Slim everyone loved. The Slim who sang and played the guitar.

"Slim, what do you mean?" Dan asked. "We've got . . ."

But Slim interrupted him and there was mockery in his voice as he spoke.

" 'You've got,' " he mimicked. "You've got nothing. Nothing but trouble! If I'd known you were thinking of such a thing!"

Dan didn't know what to say. What could Slim mean?

"You don't understand," Dan said and then repeated it. "You don't understand."

"I don't understand?" Slim asked. "Well, if I don't who does, I'd like to know. 'You've got a farm!' You're in debt to the Interests for the rest of your lives, that's what you are! Just like me and everybody else in North Dakota. 'You've got a farm!'"

"It's a homestead," Dan tried to explain. "We . . ."

But Slim interrupted him again.

"Do you think I don't know?" Slim asked bitterly. "For a year I've been seeing people come out to this God-forsaken place and mortgage their lives to get a start. You never get a start. You never get out of debt. You just get in deeper and deeper and they take everything. You think I don't know? Why do you suppose you haven't been hearing from me?"

"I don't know, Slim."

Dan's voice sounded strange, even to himself. In the face of Slim's avalanche of bitterness, he didn't know what to say.

"What's the matter? What's wrong, Slim?"

"Everything, that's all! Well, you got yourselves into it. Don't look to me to get you out."

Then Slim was hurrying away from him, off into the darkness toward the railway station and the weird whistle and clanging bell of the night train. Dan started to follow him, but his feet stopped walking. Slim wouldn't even listen to him. He didn't understand at all. He didn't know anything about Gramps and the money . . . or about Pa!

At the thought of Pa, Dan started after his brother. Slim would have to listen. He must know about Pa. He must explain about the Interests too. What were they? Who were they? Jim Jackson had said he was in debt up to his eyebrows to the Interests . . .

Dan started to run. The long, mournful whistle of the train warned him that Slim might soon be gone. Where? To Wil-

—28—

liston? At the station he hurried along beside the coaches. Men were getting off with wives and children and luggage, just as he and Pa and Mom had done, two nights before.

Lanterns waved on the station platform. Sparks from the engine shot into the night, glowing red and gold through the swirling snow. A row of lighted pictures, framed in black, the windows of the coaches seemed.

"Slim!"

It was just a choked whisper as Dan hurried from coach to coach in the confusion and the snow-filled half light.

3. Dakota Twister

CRAZY-QUILT patches of white snow and blue water lay on the grey prairie. Like the flat palm of a giant hand, reaching forever for the horizon, was this North Dakota land. All day the settlers had driven south and west, and never a change in the desert of dead grass, rustling in the wind ahead of them and behind them. Gone were the steep, sheltering hills that towered above Minot. It was hard to believe they existed at all.

Now Ike Sheets was pulling up, stopping for the night.

Dan hadn't liked to have Ike take the lead, but Ike had been out on the prairie before. He said he knew the way. Dan didn't, nor the Nelsons, nor the Jacksons. Ike had located the mounds of earth the surveyors raised when they marked off the sections, and the stones they had placed on each mound bearing inscriptions in red chalk. Each time he'd passed a marker he had signalled to the wagons behind.

"See?" he'd called out. "Like I said. Five mile." Or "Ten mile." Now they'd covered more than twenty miles and the sun was setting. The deep boom and beat of the prairie chicken's spring song, that had echoed across the plains all day, was infrequent now and the wind was quieting too. It was almost frightening, with night coming on, for there were no trees to promise protection, no hill or rocky ledge to shelter them, no place to hide.

Ike Sheets was hauling part of the lumber Mom had bought and her crate of chickens was perched on top of his load. He had bought nothing in Minot except a team and wagon and a supply of beans and flour, coffee and bacon. Behind him came Mom and Pa with the heaviest load. Next was Dan with the household goods and part of the farm machinery. And tied behind his wagon was his black and shining Prince, pressed into service to haul the seeder.

Trailing behind the Osbornes came the Jacksons. Their one wagon hauled all their belongings and the plow and harrow and seeder Jim had bought. Last came the Nelsons' three wagons, with Mrs. Nelson bringing up the rear. Chris and his sister Petra rode with Mrs. Nelson and talked for her when there was need, for she spoke no English. They had all the cattle.

"No need of slowing everyone down because of the cows," Ike Sheets had said. "One wagon otta take all of 'em and figger on an extry day for the trip." So Dan hadn't seen much of Mrs. Nelson or Petra, for they were soon trailing behind.

It wasn't Mrs. Nelson, nor the tow-headed, oval-faced Petra who was on Dan's mind as he brought his team to a stop. It was Slim. He hadn't been able to find Slim at the railway station; hadn't been able to tell him about Pa. All day he'd gone over his conversation with his brother, thinking of the

-31-

things he should have said and remembering what Slim had said. He'd talk to the Jacksons tonight when Mom wasn't around and ask Jim about the Interests. Meantime he couldn't tell Mom that he'd seen Slim. He couldn't let her know how Slim had acted. "Don't count on me to help you out," Slim had said. That would hurt Mom.

As soon as the wagons halted she was busy.

"You kids gather buffalo chips for a fire," she directed Eddie and Grace. "Dan, you be sure to hobble the horses first off, so they don't get away. Then help me get Pa out of the wagon."

They lifted him carefully and set him in his wheel chair close by the fire. Dan thought he looked tired, but when Mom asked if he was all right he nodded his head and patted her arm with his good right hand.

There was comfort in the aroma of coffee and frying bacon. Punkin yapped with joy as he raced with Eddie and Grace, and Mom's cheerful assurance would uplift anyone's spirits.

"This is a good land, Dan," she said as she watched the cloud formations changing the amber sunset. "We'll make out, with the Lord's help."

Dan strolled off to the Jacksons' wagon as soon as he had finished supper. Already they had spread blankets under the wagon and were banking their fire, and the air was spiced with the smell of smoke.

"Thought we'd turn in early," Jim said. "With a good start in the morning we figger to reach our land afore noon tomorrow. But set a spell and visit."

"Yes, do stay," Mrs. Jackson urged. "I wisht your Mom had come along too."

"Likely you'll see a lot of her, once we get settled," Dan said. "I recall she said something about being neighborly, back in Minot."

That was it. He'd try to keep the conversation on Minot and the things that had happened there. That way he could lead up to the question he wanted answered. So he talked about prices and how much Mom had paid for things.

"I didn't know farm machinery cost so much," Dan said. "Fifty-five dollars for a gang plow and $25 for a harrow."

"And $120 for a seeder," Jim said with a long groan. "But you folks come out here well-to-do. We've got to make it all with our bare hands, Ida an' me."

"It'll be my bare hands too," Dan said. "Mine and Mom's. Where's the difference?"

"You folks ain't mortgaged to start. Neither you nor the Nelsons. But take us. Ike Sheets too, if he ever does anything with his land . . ." Jim hesitated.

"What is Ike figuring on doing?" Mrs. Jackson asked. "He ain't got no farmin' tools at all."

"He offered to haul our lumber, for the loan of our plow and harrow after we get through using them," Dan explained. "He told Mom he's only going to break the 10 acres the law requires each year, so it doesn't matter much if he's late with his plowing. But you folks now. You've got to get as much land under cultivation as you can, same as us, don't you?"

"Don't we!" Jim repeated and in the dusk Dan could see his jaw jut out as he rubbed both hands across his stubble-coated chin. "Man, we've got to. We've got to get crops this very first year or . . . Wait! What's that?"

It was the thud of a horse's hooves pounding the prairie. What horse was that? All of the horses were hobbled so they couldn't run.

Dan was on his feet in an instant, staring in disbelief and mounting alarm.

"It's yours, ain't it?" Jim asked as the animal raced off across the plain. "It's your black, ain't it?"

Dan didn't stop to answer.

"Prince," he cried out. "Prince, come back here!"

He started running, but he knew before he had gone a dozen steps that he couldn't catch Prince on foot. In desperation he raced back to his own wagons and the other hobbled animals. He'd ride one of them after Prince.

Mom was running toward the horses too, trailed by Eddie and Grace.

"How could he have gotten away, Dan?" she called. "Didn't you fasten the hobbles good?"

"Of course I did," Dan answered sharply, as he grabbed for a bridle.

"You'll never catch him, Dan," Mom warned but this time he paid no heed to her. He must catch Prince. Already his horse was off on the darkening prairie, scarce in sight.

"I tell you you'll never catch him, Dan," Mom called again as he rode away. "Don't follow him too far from the wagons and get lost. Night's coming on."

Dan slapped the side of the horse he was riding, but the animal was tired from a day's hauling and made no attempt to gallop. And Dan, without experience at riding, slipped and slid from side to side on the broad bay back, as the horse ran jerkily over the uneven ground.

"Prince!" Dan kept calling. "Prince! Come, Prince!"

He could see the big black, a mile away now, and still running. Prince was built to run, too. As Dan jolted along he knew that Mom was right. He couldn't catch Prince. Perhaps he was driving his horse farther away by this futile chase. Slowly he turned around and headed back to the wagons.

It was all Dan could do to keep back the tears. His horse! The very first thing he had ever owned! How could Prince have gotten loose? He'd hobbled all of the animals securely.

-34-

Someone . . . certainly someone must have unbuckled the hobble.

"Mom, did you see anyone near the horses?" Dan asked as he slid to the ground and took the hobble she held out to him. "Did you see Tom Sheets anywhere about?"

"Now, Dan, don't you go accusing anyone of a trick like that," Mom said piling fresh chips on the fire.

"You didn't answer me," Dan said and waited for her to tell him, straight out, yes or no.

"Tom was here a few minutes after you went to the Jacksons' wagon, but he was back at his own rig long before Prince took off," Mom told him. "There wasn't anyone near the horses when Prince took a lunge and started to run. I saw him at the very moment."

"I hobbled him just like the rest," Dan said. "Someone must have unbuckled the hobble."

Mom shook her head. "He could have broken the hobble if it was weak in any way, Dan," she said. "He could have been bit by a snake and so took a lunge and broken loose. I always thought snakes were in their holes by sunset though."

It was a possible explanation.

"We don't know what varmint there may be out on this prairie by night," Dan admitted.

But he didn't think it was a night prowler of any kind that had terrified his horse. Prince had been raised right out on these prairies. It was something else. Dan couldn't talk about it any more. Miserably he took himself to the pallet Mom had made for him under his wagon, beside the kids who already had been put to bed.

It seemed to Dan he didn't sleep at all that night, what with thinking of Slim and his horse. With the first streak of light he was up, building a fire and peering into the vermilion sunrise. There was a dark spot against the morning sky. Was it Prince or a cloud speck? He stared and wondered. Would Prince come back to the wagon train or return to Minot? Where would he go?

One by one the Jacksons and Nelsons roused themselves and started fires. Nels and Jim came to Dan's wagon before the trek resumed, but Ike and Tom Sheets stayed by their own camp fire.

"Pa says your horse more'n likely will follow along somewhere near the rest of the animals," Nels said. "He may stay a mile or more away, but Pa thinks he's more likely to follow along with the rest than to wander off by himself."

"I hope he's right," Dan replied miserably as he hitched the bays to his wagon.

Sometimes the route followed buffalo trails, but more often there was no track at all to follow, that day. By mid-morning Ike Sheets was shouting information back to the wagons behind.

"Almost there. Five mile more!"

A little later he called to the others again.

"See them trees ahead? A clump of willows on somebody's land."

They came first to Ike's claim. Across the line, where there soon would be a road beaten down by their own wagon wheels, Jim Jackson's land was located. Adjoining Sheets' quarter section was the Osborne's land and beyond it the Nelsons'.

"Those willows are on your farm, by the look," Mr. Nelson called to Dan. "You drew the prize."

"What prize?" Dan asked bitterly, but as he said it he understood. The little clump of a scant half-dozen willows and two or three poplar trees meant water near the surface. He'd heard the men in line back in Minot talking about wells, and how deep some homesteaders had dug before they struck water. He wouldn't have any trouble getting a well if those trees were on his land.

Mr. Nelson stopped alongside Mom's wagon as she drew to a halt by the willows.

"We've all agreed to put up your house first," he said. "Jackson'll be along as soon as he unloads his stuff, and Sheets with your lumber. So you decide where you'd like to build and we'll get started as soon as we eat."

The willows were at the far end of the Osborne land and back from the line where the road would run. Mom looked toward a slight rise in the ground just beyond the trees.

"Water'll drain off from there when the snow melts in spring," she said so Dan drove his team to the spot and she followed.

When Ike Sheets came with the lumber, he had Jim Jackson with him. Tom had been left behind and Dan wondered why. Was Tom afraid to face him? Not one word did Ike say about the missing horse. It didn't seem natural to Dan.

"I was a-thinkin' as I rode along," Ike said to Mom, looking past her rather than directly at her. "I figgered how it would be easier for me to borry Jackson's plow, beings as how he's goin' to live right acrost the road from me. So if it's all the same to you, you can pay for this haulin' job with a little lumber. I can use it for doors and window jambs on the sod shanty Tom and I aim to build."

Mom looked from Sheets to his wagon and her lumber. It seemed to Dan that she was really taking stock of the hulking man for the first time and seeing everything now—the buttons missing from his clothes, the dirty, broken finger nails, the pouchy features and drooping lids that half hid blue-grey eyes.

–37–

Perhaps he sensed it too, for he shifted uneasily and fumbled in the pockets of his baggy overcoat, finally bringing out a stained corn cob pipe.

"Mind if I smoke?" he asked, pounding the pipe against the heel of his shoe.

Mom said no, and surveyed the load of lumber on the Sheets wagon. Dan didn't think she had bought more than she needed, and he wondered if she would agree to this new bargain.

"Did you take the lumber off already?" she asked and there was an unusual sharpness to her voice. "It appears to me you did."

"About enough for the door, yes," Sheets admitted. "Now if you ain't got enough left so as I could eke out a couple of window jambs, it's still a bargain an' no obligation."

Mom had a way of pressing her lips tight together when she was trying not to say something she'd be sorry for. Dan knew that look and he saw it now as she surveyed the Sheets' wagon. In a way, he was glad. It was just as well if Mom understood this Sheets outfit, at the start.

"We'll see how we make out when we get to building," Mom said. "Now, Dan, help me with Pa. This trip has been tiring enough for him. And let's get the lumber unloaded right away."

With Mr. Nelson taking charge, the men made fast work of the house-raising. The skirring sound of saws, the ring of hammers against the heavy spikes, was businesslike and re-assuring. On the knoll beside the house Mom's furniture was spread out, ready to be moved inside. There were the three brass beds, shining in the sun; the big oak dining room set and the dark red over-stuffed parlor furniture that had come from Gramps' house. Propped between barrels of dishes was the crate that held his big Grandfather's clock. By another noon it would all be settled neatly in the Osborne's own home. Then it would be Dan's turn to help the Nelsons and Jim Jackson, and even Ike Sheets with their building.

The Nelsons had bought lumber for their house and barns too, but Jim as well as Ike was planning to build a sod shanty. As the men worked, Jim was dickering too. If there was any extra lumber, he'd like enough for a door and window jambs, and even a floor. He'd put in an extra day's work at the Nelsons, just as soon as he had his land broke. Dan was glad when Mr. Nelson agreed to Jim's offer. He didn't like to think Ike Sheets would have a better sod house than Jim and Ida Jackson.

Now and then Dan looked from his work to see what Mom was doing. The kids had gathered big piles of buffalo chips and plainly she was preparing an evening meal for everyone. Sitting in his wheel chair, bundled in blankets, Pa nodded or shook his head as she talked to him. Sometime in the afternoon Ida Jackson joined them to help with the work. Then laughter and the shrill screams of the youngsters as they raced with Punkin, mingled with hammer blows.

Smoked ham boiling over the open fire, and dried fruit simmering in simple syrup promised a good meal that night. The smells that came to the men were mouth-watering. Dan never could remember when Mom couldn't whip up a good meal somehow!

It was near dusk and the men were preparing to quit for the night when Mrs. Nelson's wagon came into sight. At first Dan gave it only a glance. He'd be glad to see Chris again, of course. But as the rig with its rear guard of cattle came nearer, Dan looked again and called excitedly to Nels.

"Do you make out anything?" he asked anxiously.

Nels lifted a hand to shield his eyes and nodded slowly.

"Let's ride out to meet them," he said.

As the boys started for the horses, Jim and Mr. Nelson also stopped work to peer at the on-coming wagon. Dan caught the trace of a smile on Mr. Nelson's face and stopped for a second, not knowing whether to voice his hope or not.

"I'm sure it is," Mr. Nelson said. "And right glad I am."

Dan knew then, for sure. Chris and Mrs. Nelson had Prince with them. Somehow they had caught him.

Bouncing uncomfortably, Dan urged the plow horse to run, and every step brought reassurance. As he passed Ike Sheets' claim he glanced at the wall of the sod shanty which Tom had started. Beyond it Tom had built a fire, and was leaning over it pretending not to see Dan and Nels. Dan had a notion to stop and see what Tom would say to him, but Nels was pressing behind him, and a mile ahead was the approaching wagon, with Prince. He couldn't wait to find out how Chris had caught his horse.

"Chris," Dan called excitedly as he rode alongside, scarcely nodding to Mrs. Nelson and Petra. "How did you get him?"

"Petra did it," Chris replied and as Dan again asked how, the youngest of the Nelsons smiled with pride and friendliness.

"With the feed bag," Petra told him, leaning out of the wagon. Her bright red bonnet was hanging by its ribbons down her back, and the fading sunlight reddened her heavy gold braids. Petra, Dan guessed, wasn't more than thirteen or fourteen years old at most. She was a slender girl, and in build and manners she was quite unlike her husky, matter-of-fact brothers. But she had Chris' friendly manner.

"Petra can coax anything her way, man or beast," Chris said with a note of admiration for his sister.

"How you talk!" she said but her eyes twinkled with pleasure. "I just held out the bag of oats. That's what he wanted. And petted him a little until I could slip a halter on. How did he get away?"

"That's what I'd like to find out," Dan said and repeated the story of what had happened. "Was his hobble broken or unbuckled?"

"It was busted," Chris replied. "I figured he must have broken away from you when you first hobbled him."

"That wasn't how it happened," Dan said. "I figured he must have been let loose by someone, for meanness. But if the hobble was broken, well, I don't know what to think."

Prince tossed his head and whinnied softly as Dan rode back and fell in line beside him. Slowly the outfit moved toward the glowing fires ahead, Dan staying behind with his horse. He hoped Tom Sheets was looking as they passed the sod shanty wall. Somehow Dan still felt that Tom at least knew how Prince had gotten away.

The men finished the Osborne house the next day and Mr. Nelson taught Dan how to dig a well and build a guard wall around it, and a watering trough for the animals. There was no pump, but a pail and rope brought the water up just fine. One quick flip turned the pail on its side as it hit the water, and did the trick. It pleased Dan to see how easily he caught on.

"It's a fine spring well you've got there, Dan," Mr. Nelson said. "Likely all the neighbors will be watering at your well for a few weeks. It won't be so easy for the rest of us to get water."

That was how it was, too. Each night at sunset the horses and cattle from the little cluster of farms were driven to the well beside the willows to water. Each family built a stoneboat, and hauled back a barrel of water for cooking and washing.

The second night Tom came with Jim, bringing the Sheets'

team. An old galvanized tub was crowded onto Jim's stone-boat, apparently for water for the Sheets' use.

"Ike Sheets really practices being neighborly," Dan muttered to Chris who was at the well with him, as they watched Jim's stoneboat bumping along slowly.

"I wonder what Tom'll have to say," Chris said slowly. Dan wondered too. This was the first time he had met Tom, face to face, since the night Tom had turned on him as they stood in line in front of the Minot Land Office.

Tom held his own horses back for Jim to water first.

"You go ahead," he said. Then with unexpected friendliness he turned to Dan.

"Paw calls this the finest waterin' place on the prairie," he said. "You sure were lucky."

"I guess so," Dan replied, looking straight at Tom. "In more ways than one."

But Tom ignored the remark.

"Getting on your land tomorrow?" he asked. "Frost's out of the ground now and everybody's got a roof over their heads."

Dan found it difficult to understand Tom's changed attitude. Was it because he felt the score was evened when Prince got loose?

"We'll be starting on the land first thing in the morning," Dan answered after a moment's hesitation. "Me right here at this end of our land, and Chris and Nels on theirs," and he turned to look back at the spread of acres separating the two farms.

"Chris, that's a funny cloud," he said changing the subject abruptly. "They sure have the most sky and the wildest clouds out here I ever saw. Look at that one."

It was like a giant funnel, its spout on the horizon and its spread high in the heavens. A huge, black funnel it was, the sky around it a sickly green, changing to copper and bronze and purple all at once. Dan stared at it in wonderment until Tom's frightened cry made him turn back to look at the others.

"It's a twister!" Tom gasped and his mouth fell open as he stared at it. "A twister! Nothing can stand up against it! Get down! Get down!"

Tom threw himself onto the ground, face down. Dan stared at Chris, then back at the cloud. It was moving fast, headed toward them, holding its shape as it came on.

The wind was rising, black dirt swirling in the sky, blowing up suddenly from nowhere. Thunder rolled over the whole vast prairie, booming and exploding. The cows were lying down, the horses turning their tails toward the wind. Chris had followed Tom's example and was lying face down, his fingers gripping at the dead grass.

Dan had been holding Prince by the halter. Now as surprise changed to terror he threw his arms around his horse's neck.

"Down, Prince!" he shouted above the wind, pulling at the long black mane. "Down!"

The horse tossed its head wildly, then suddenly lay down. Dan dropped to the earth beside him and clung to Prince's neck as stinging pellets of rain beat against him, and yellow skeins of lightning crackled and flashed overhead, from horizon to horizon. Peering from this shelter, Dan could see the breast of the cyclone, 200 or more feet in the sky. A great, swirling mass of dirt and tumbleweeds, feathers and fur, all boiling together in the terrible cone-shaped cloud. Dan's eyes filled with dust, the gale ripped at his clothing, and he clung to Prince gasping for breath. Something black was flying over his head but he couldn't see what it was. Didn't dare to look.

In seconds the twister passed. Dan felt the wind lessening its pull on his clothing, the roar abated and he raised his head to stare around him. His house was still standing, but two of the poplar trees were down, the guard rail had been torn from the well, and the water trough was strewn in broken bits 100 feet or more from the well.

Most frightening of all was the sight of Jim Jackson. He was standing between his two horses, one arm around the neck of each, his trousers ripped from his legs and flapping ahead of him in the wind. Like a frozen monument he stood, staring toward his own sod shanty which had been nearer the center of the cyclone than the willows and the well. Jim's face was ashen and his lips were moving but no sounds came. With one sudden, animal-like leap he mounted one of the horses, jerked furiously at the neckrope of the other, and, leaving stone boat and broken barrel behind, he raced for his house.

Dan and Chris, getting up slowly, stared after him dumb-founded.

"He sure was scared," Dan said rubbing the dirt from his eyes and spitting it out of his mouth. "I thought I was scared."

"He's got reason," Tom replied. "If his farmin' tools is busted, so's he."

"What do you mean?" Dan asked quickly. Tom's words had an ominous sound.

"He's mortgaged for everything," Tom replied. "First mort-gage on his land to buy his tools and horses. Took a chattel mortgage on his horses to buy his harness. My Paw says the Interests'll take everything he gets from now till he proves up, and after that too. He don't dare lose nothin'."

"How does your Paw know?" Dan demanded, suddenly

-44-

resentful. Dan liked Jim Jackson. "Who're the Interests, anyway? That's what I'd like to know."

"Don't you know?" Tom asked. Then with unconcealed pride he explained it.

"The Interests are Jim Hill and his railroad, and the milling men in Minneapolis. They own North Dakota."

"How do you know so much about it?" Dan insisted.

"Because my Paw's got connections," Tom shot back, all friendliness suddenly gone.

Dan turned from Tom in sudden fury. "Come on, Chris. Let's see what's happened to Jim."

But Chris held back. "I can't," he protested. "Pa and Nels will be needing me. Our stuff's blown from here all the way home to Norway, like enough."

Dan looked at his own buildings. They were standing. The wagons had careened down the slope into the cluster of trees and the seeder was piled against them. Well, if anything was broken he would have to fix it later. But Jim! The Interests did own Jim, then, just like Slim had said. This was what Slim had thought would happen to him and Pa and Mom.

With a quick jump Dan was on Prince's back, galloping across the prairie after Jim.

4. *Straight Furrows*

THE tornado had struck Jim Jackson's sod shanty with lethal force. One wall was blown out completely. Sod blocks that had covered the wooden rafters were strewn for rods across the prairie. When Dan rode up, Ida Jackson was gathering pots and pans and household goods back into the doubtful shelter of three sagging walls. She wiped her face with the back of a dust-streaked hand smearing dirt and tears across her cheeks. Jim scarcely looked at either Ida or Dan. He was tugging with all his great strength at his seeder which the twister had driven up against his plow. A full quarter of a mile from the house his wagon had come to a stop. His harrow, spikes deep in the earth, alone was untouched by the storm.

"Is anything busted, Jim?" Dan asked as he gave a hand to the task of untangling plow and seeder.

"I guess not, thank the Lord," Jim replied and there was no question that he meant it.

"If your tools are safe we can re-build the house easy enough," Dan assured him. Jim nodded and with another shove got his seeder back on the ground.

"This teaches us one thing," Jim said. "There's gotta be shelter for tools and animals as well as human beings. I've got to build barns of some kind, money or no money. And I've got to lay better roofs."

"You can build sod barns as well as a sod house," Dan replied. "The neighbors will help."

"I can't get too indebted to the neighbors," Jim answered wiping the dust from his eyes and rubbing disgustedly at his torn trouser legs. "I'm so in debt now I can't take on no more."

"How do you mean?" Dan asked. "You've said that before."

Jim started toward his wagon and Dan followed.

"You know how much cash money me and Ida had when we hit Minot?" Jim asked, then answered his own question. "Fifty dollars, that's what we had. Fifty dollars and her household stuff. We drove up from Nebrasky with another couple who had no more'n us, except for a team and wagon. I wisht we'd had that much more ourselves."

"Then you did have to go in debt to the Interests, like you said back in Minot," Dan said. "Is the bank the Interests?"

"Yes and no," Jim told him. "I borrowed at the Loan Office, but the feller there told me he gets the money from the bank and the bank gets it in Minneapolis. The Loan Office charged me 12% interest on the $800 I borrowed, and dated the mortgage back six months so I owed them $48 right off. The feller said he had to do it to protect himself, in case I didn't pay up on time. Then the feller who give the chattel mortgage on my horses charged $50 for fixin' up that loan. Said he had to do it. Same story. Between 'em they got $100 of the $800 I borrowed."

It was more than Dan could understand, all at once. But Jim went on with his story, pouring out his worries for the first time.

"I tell you, Dan, them fellers in Minot is all in cahoots. The man at the Loan Office tells me where to go for my horses and tools and how to get the harness. I bet the feller he sent me to knew just how much I got, and how much I had left after I'd bought the animals and all."

Dan gave a shove at the wagon. He'd never heard of business deals like these.

"I don't want you should say a word to Ida about this," Jim warned, his voice dropping needlessly. "I don't want her to start worryin'. She thinks I've got money left of the $800, but I ain't. Barely enough to buy the food we'll need from now 'till harvest."

A sick feeling welled up inside Dan as Jim talked. This was what was meant by "The Interests." This was what Slim had feared and warned against; what Ike Sheets had been talking about. And Tom had been right about Jim's situation.

"Jim, what connection has Ike Sheets got with the Interests?" Dan asked. "Tom said his old man has connections."

Jim examined his wagon before answering. He lifted the tongue and found it unbroken. One pull and the wheels responded. Again Dan gave a hand and they began hauling the wagon back toward Jim's ruined shanty.

"I don't know for sure what connections he's got," Jim said after the wagon was rolling smoothly. "He tells me he used to work for Jim Hill and the Great Northern Railroad, back in St. Paul. Jim Hill is the King Pin of 'em all. He put the Great Northern through and he owns most of it, I guess. Whether Ike Sheets ever seen Jim Hill or not, I don't know. But he knows the feller in the Loan Office and he makes it a point to find out all about everybody's business. I don't know if it's just natural curiosity or somethin' more'n that."

"I don't like him. Nor Tom much, either," Dan said.

"I don't myself," Jim agreed, "but I sure don't want Ike for an enemy. I don't want to be beholdin' to him, neither. That's why I figger I'll let the work on the house an' barns wait until I can git at it myself. I can't ask the rest of the neighbors to give me a hand and not ask him, too. And I can't wait no longer to git on the land. Seedin's got to be done by the end of April."

Dan knew that was true. Mom had been quoting the literature put out by the Agricultural College ever since they'd started plans for coming to North Dakota. In March they could start breaking the land. By May first all crops had to be in. Dan knew it by heart.

"You folks can sleep at our place until you get your roof up again," Dan offered. "It'll be all right with Mom."

Ida, who had come to meet them and heard the offer, shook her head. "That's right kind of you, Dan, but we ain't afraid of sleepin' under the sky. I'd rather stay close by our stuff now. There's just no tellin' what'll happen next."

"Seems like there couldn't be anything more," Dan said. Now that the first terror of the cyclone was over, it didn't seem so bad. "Things ought to go along easier for all of us now, for a spell at least."

That was how it was, too. Each morning Dan took his team and plow out onto the land soon after sunrise. The grey prairie was greening, and the sod turned easily and lay in black rows behind him. It had been no trick at all to lay a straight, even furrow, once Dan had the hang of it. As soon as he had a good start, Mom had followed him with the harrow, breaking the sod into loose, soft chunks ready for seeding. She came into the field every morning as soon as breakfast was over and the milking done.

Dan could have sung for joy as the field grew, black and fine and larger each night, only it took all his strength and wind to hold the plow firm and guide the horses. Overhead the sun shone warm and bright. Endless battalions of wild geese, each in V formation, honked their way north into Canada. And Grace and Eddie sang for him. Barefooted, they tagged behind the plow, Grace with her bedraggled doll under her arm.

"You should take your shoes off, too," Eddie told Dan. "It's like a sponge. I've got a soft, black sponge under my feet and a soft, white sponge covering me."

"What soft white sponge?" Grace asked. "There's nothing over you but air."

"There is so," Eddie contradicted. "Soft, white spongy clouds. I can lie on the prairie and reach up to them. I can shut my eyes and go right up into them."

"You cannot!" Grace contradicted. "He's making things up, Dan. Make him stop it."

But Eddie ignored her. "They're cumulus clouds," he announced. "The wind blows them along up in the sky."

Dan glanced over his shoulder at his little brother. Eddie was slender and dark and with a start Dan realized that he was very much like Slim, except that his eyes were blue. What had he been saying? Where had he learned that word, *cumulus?*

"How do you know what kind of clouds they are, Eddie?" Dan asked.

"Papa told me," Eddie answered undisturbed. "See that bird over there with the streaks and speckles down his back? That's a meadow lark. He's going to build a nest and it'll have a cover over it."

Dan felt his brows contracting into a frown. Was Eddie really making up all of the things he was saying?

"How do you know what kind of a bird it is? Or what kind of a nest it'll build?" Dan asked.

"Papa told me that, too. And the little blue flowers that grew right up beside the snow banks when we first got here. They're pasque flowers. Mom called them crocuses but they're pasque flowers."

Dan stopped the horses for a breather. He knew the flowers all right. Soft, fuzzy and delicate blue they were with a sweet musk scent. The prairie had been dotted with them only a few days ago, but had Pa really told Eddie they were pasque flowers? Dan glanced cautiously at Grace. A little grandmother she looked in her blue and white gingham dress, her tidy pigtails, and the stolid stance of her sturdy legs.

"Papa told him all right," she said as though reading Dan's mind. "Eddie can understand everything Papa says. I can't though."

"I don't see why not," Eddie replied calmly. "All you have to do is listen. Slowly."

The conversation bothered Dan. He hadn't been listening to his father much, he knew. Nor trying to talk to him, either. Dan had been too tired, when the long day ended, to do anything but eat his supper and go to bed. Twelve hours a day he spent out on the land, plowing as much as possible each day. Just before sunset Mom would leave the harrowing and go back to milk the cows and get supper. Then she and Dan would both drop into their beds, leaving Eddie and Grace to clean up. Dan realized he hadn't said a dozen words a day to his father, and hadn't expected an answer. Well, he'd try to do better, beginning that very night. He'd find out whether Pa could talk to Eddie or not.

With a long sigh Dan picked up the plow handles again, and his mind wandered back to Slim. If Slim were here to help, they'd get the land broken and a good crop in this first year. But it went so slowly, working alone. The Nelsons had more than twice as much land broken as he or Jim Jackson. If only Slim were home, or Pa able to be up and working.

That evening, at the supper table, Dan spoke directly to his father. He'd tried to do it as he washed up. Bending over the basin so he could avoid looking at his father, he had tried to speak but Pa had wheeled himself away toward the table. Now Dan kept his eyes on his plate and slowly mashed gravy into the boiled potatoes Mom had prepared. He hadn't eaten a bite because he wasn't sure he could swallow. He wondered if he'd be able to say the words he had so carefully decided upon.

"Pa, have you any way of figuring how much land I've got plowed?"

It seemed to Dan that the question sounded natural enough, once he'd got it out. He was sure his mother's eyes were on him as he deliberately cut the crisp salt pork into little pieces. Eddie and Grace, fortunately, went on eating without noticing the silence that followed the question.

If Pa could talk to Eddie, certainly he could answer Dan, but he didn't. Should Dan ask the question again? Then Eddie's words came back to him. "All you have to do is listen. *Slowly*."

Dan took a bite of his supper. He wouldn't repeat the question. Pa had heard it all right.

"About . . . 65 . . . acres." Pa said it slowly, but Dan could understand every word.

He kept his eyes on his plate. "I figure I've got about another week for plowing, then I'll have to start seeding. I wonder how much I can get cultivated this spring."

After he'd said it he almost held his breath for fear Mom would answer, but she didn't. No one answered for a long time, then Pa said, clear enough for anyone who was listening, "Eighty . . . acres."

Dan ran his hands through his long red hair, slicked down now for the dinner table, and heaved a sigh.

"It's not enough, Pa," he said but he felt elated. And he couldn't help smiling. He'd had a real conversation with his father for the first time since the horrible day on the train when the illness had struck Pa silent. It seemed as though his father was smiling too. But the next moment Dan's happiness faded for his father said something more and Dan couldn't understand a word of it. He opened his mouth to question, but stopped and tried to recall the sounds his father had made. Tried to make words of them. Then Pa spoke again and this time he said only one word.

"Garden."

"He wants you should plow up a plot for a garden," Eddie said between bites. "I should have told you before. Papa's been saying he and I could get the seeds in with a hoe if you'd plow up a garden plot for us. I just forgot to tell you."

"I'll plow a garden, Pa," Dan promised. "I'll plow it tonight. The moon's bright as day."

Dan forgot how tired he had been as he harnessed the horses again and started the furrows for a garden plot near the well. After a bit Mom came out and walked beside him.

"I was right happy about what you did tonight, Dan," she said. "We can get Pa to talking again, with a little patience."

"Sure we can," Dan agreed. "It was Eddie who made me realize it. He's kept talking with Pa until he can understand him. I should have thought of it before."

"I've been too tired to think, myself," Mom admitted. "And not a little worried too."

"Worried?" Dan asked.

"Have you figured what we can expect to realize from crops this fall?"

Dan had to admit that he hadn't.

"We can't get more than 80 acres under cultivation, if that much," Mom said. "The Nelsons will have that much wheat and about another 80 in to flax, but we can't do as much as three men, Dan."

Dan knew the Nelsons were planting flax too. Wheat and some oats for winter feeding was the best he could hope to do.

"If we average 15 bushels to the acre and wheat sells for 65¢, we'll make less than $725 if you can get 75 acres into wheat," Mom said. "We still have a harvester to buy and that's $125. Grain bags and binder twine and such will cost another $15 or $20. We've got to buy a mowing machine and a horse rake and a hay rack to lay away hay for winter feed. We won't have enough left to more than feed ourselves this first year, Dan."

The way Mom figured it, they'd be as bad off as Jim Jackson and there were more of them to feed. They had no debt to pay though, and Dan reminded his mother that the income at least was all theirs.

"I thank the Lord for that every night," Mom answered. "We've neglected having family prayers this past month because I didn't know if I could keep awake long enough to read the Good Book. But I haven't neglected to thank the Lord and to ask for His guidance, too. I don't know if what I heard today is His word or not."

"What do you mean, Mom?" Dan asked.

"When Petra Nelson came over she just happened to mention that a man off down southwest of here has sheep. He'll sell some of them but Ike Sheets said nobody should buy."

"Sheep?" Dan repeated. What, exactly, was Mom wanting sheep for?

"We could pasture them all summer on the land we can't get plowed," Mom explained. "In the fall there'd be the wool to sell and mutton too."

"Wouldn't we have to fence off the pasture land?" Dan asked. "They'd get into the neighbor's grain if we didn't."

"We'd have to fence," Mom admitted.

"What would that cost?" Dan asked.

Mom ignored the question. "Ike Sheets is against bringing sheep into grain country but I can't see his reasoning," she went on. "So as soon as you get the seeding done I want you to go see what we can buy sheep for, and what fencing would cost."

"What about the money, Mom?" Dan pressed. "Have you got enough left to buy sheep and fencing and the tools we've got to get?"

"I might have to get a small loan," Mom admitted. "I haven't spent all our money, but I don't know what it'll take to buy sheep and fencing."

Suddenly Dan was wet with sweat and frightened as he'd never been in all his life.

"Don't get no loan, Mom!" he urged and his hands gripped the handles of the plow. "Don't go into debt to the Interests!"

"Why Dan, what do you mean?" Mom asked in surprise. "You sound as though a loan was a sin or something."

"It's just as bad," Dan told her. "It's worse. I know!"

"How do you know?" Mom demanded. "What do you know?"

He couldn't tell her about Slim but he could tell her about Jim Jackson.

"We aren't in the same fix as Jim Jackson at all," Mom assured him when he had finished telling Jim's story. "And I don't take any stock in what the Sheetses say."

Dan stopped the horses. He just couldn't go on plowing. In the clear, white moonlight he faced his mother. She looked at him intently, surprise and annoyance showing plainly in her face.

"Mom, I heard the same thing in Minot," Dan told her earnestly. "When I was standing in line, and at the livery stable. You don't know how the men talked, Mom!"

She stood, hands on her hips, staring at him. Dan realized that he had never crossed his mother before, but he had to do it now.

"I'd rather we got along with nothing until I can get another crop in next year," he pressed. "We won't go hungry. We'll plant this garden and raise our food."

"Well, Dan, you do make it sound right frightening," Mom admitted at last. "I didn't say we had to do it. There's no harm in finding out what it would cost, though."

Dan could agree to that.

"All right, Mom, I'll go," he promised. "As soon as the crops are in. But I think you should let me know how much money we've got left, before we dicker for sheep or fencing. I'm dead set against bargaining for more than we can pay for."

Dan shoved hard at the plow handle as he said it. Mom

didn't realize, even now that he'd told her, what it meant to let the Interests get a hold on you, he was sure. But he knew. Jim Jackson knew. And in some way that Dan didn't understand, Slim knew better than anyone else.

Slim! There he was again. In the back of Dan's mind a vague idea began to form, then a plan.

5. *Wheat Country*

DAN stopped at the Nelsons' before starting his trip to find out about the sheep. If he could borrow a saddle that would fit Prince, the ride wouldn't be so hard. He'd hoped to buy a saddle in the fall, and a pretty new doll for Grace, and a chemistry set for Eddie, maybe. But the way Mom had figured it, there'd be no money for anything like that.

Things were worse than Mom had figured, too. Dan didn't have 80 acres under cultivation, and part of the land he'd had to put into oats to feed the horses and cows during the winter. Sheep might bring in some extra money, but Mom had finally confided that she had only $300 left. Dan was sure he couldn't buy fencing and sheep and machines for haying and harvest with no more money than that. It was a worry all right.

Petra ran to meet Dan as he rode into the Nelson yard. It was good to see her for she was always smiling like Chris, not serious like Nels. The very sight of her lightened Dan's mood.

"You're out early," she called to him. "Come in and have a cup of coffee. The boys are still eating."

"I haven't time, Petra," Dan said. "I just wanted to borrow a saddle. Do you suppose Chris or Nels would loan one?"

"That they would," Petra assured him. "Come on to the barn. Likely they'll be along."

Petra led the way, her shining braids and bright plaid skirt flying in the wind.

"Where are you going?" she asked.

"I'm headed down Williston way," Dan told her. He and Mom had agreed not to mention sheep to anyone. There were things beside sheep to be bargained for.

But Petra was not easily put off.

"What for?" she demanded.

"We've got to buy our mower and hay rack and harvester," Dan explained. "Mom thought we might do better somewhere beside Minot."

Satisfied, Petra stroked Prince's neck and rubbed her cheek against his soft nose as Dan looked at the saddles.

"When are you going to let me ride him?" she asked, teasingly.

"Soon as I come back," Dan promised.

Then the boys came to the barn and Dan had to explain his proposed trip all over.

"Better take a couple of saddle blankets, Red," Nels advised, tossing the blankets to him. "You don't know what you'll run into before you get back, and livery stables cost money."

"Wish I was going along," Chris said. "If we only had the garden in, likely I could go."

Dan was glad, this once, that he was going alone. Ordinarily he would have welcomed company on a long ride across the empty prairie, but now he had too much on his mind that he couldn't talk about.

"Mom figures she can finish the garden without me," Dan told his friends. "It's half done already, with what Pa and Eddie managed to do after I got the land plowed and harrowed."

What Pa and Eddie had done was really wonderful, Dan thought, as he rode off under a dull grey sky. Wheeling himself along, Pa had dug holes for the seed potatoes and hoed long troughs for other garden seed. There would be carrots and parsnips and turnips and onions aplenty. Root vegetables were the surest garden crop, according to the literature Mom got from the Agricultural College. Peas and tomatoes and such were in danger of being nipped by early frosts, but Mom intended to try a few rows just the same. Lettuce and radishes she'd planted too. The very thought of those vegetables was mouth-watering. The only green thing they'd had to eat in weeks was the wild vetch which Pa had discovered was safe to eat and tasty when seasoned with salt and butter.

But Dan soon forgot the garden and its promise of good things to come. Before he had been riding an hour the overcast sky let loose a flurry of snow flakes. Thicker and faster they came, and the wind rose higher. The swirling whiteness was like a feather pillow burst loose over him, and he could scarcely see beyond Prince's head. And his nose was filling with miserable sniffles, too. It was a bad day.

Dan had heard wild tales of North Dakota blizzards but he hadn't thought such storms ever came in May. Men got lost in the maze of snow and wandered in circles and froze to death within a few feet of their own doors, he'd heard. Now here he was, all alone in the middle of one, and without any very clear idea of where he was headed for. A coulee off to the southwest was all Ike Sheets had told the Nelsons. In this storm Dan didn't know whether he was going southwest or not. All he had to go by was the wind, and no way of knowing whether it had shifted. But it wasn't cold. There was no danger of freezing to death he assured himself, even as he sneezed. So he continued on in the storm.

Dan wasn't sure whether Prince's animal instinct led him to the sod shanty which he came upon, or whether by pure happenstance it lay in his path. In any event, it was suddenly in front of him, a blur of blackness in the white mist. A horse, standing close against the sheltering walls, told Dan someone was inside.

The door was a canvas flap and there was no way to knock, so Dan called out "Hello!" At once a head poked out from behind the flap and a friendly voice answered.

"Hello. Come in out of the storm."

The accent was German. Quickly Dan removed the saddle, covered Prince with one of the blankets and hobbled him.

"Some snow!" Dan said shaking it from his coat and cap as he pushed the canvas aside and entered the dimly-lighted shanty.

"Ya, some snow," the man repeated. "Come by the fire and warm yourself."

A small, round stove, glowing red with heat, was drying out the fresh sod of the walls, and an acrid smell like burning leaves in the fall, filled the room. Packing boxes served as chairs and table, and a flickering kerosene lantern furnished the only light for there were no windows. A cot was the only furniture.

As Dan's eyes adjusted to the dimness he could see that the slender man who had so readily taken him in was young, although his beard was dark and heavy. His clothing, in contrast to the barrenness of the shanty, was new and good, and two valises on the dirt floor by the cot indicated other possessions.

"Looking for your homestead?" the man asked, moving a box nearer to the welcome heat.

"No, we've got ours," Dan answered, pleased that a stranger would mistake his age. "I was looking for a man who has sheep for sale. My name is Dan Osborne and my family lives about 10 miles northeast of here. I guess it's northeast anyway. I've not been sure of my directions the last hour or so."

"I'm John Schneider," Dan's host said pronouncing his name "Yon." "We get here week before last. Coulee's southwest of here all right. We come by it."

"We?" Dan asked.

"Ya, me and my brother Ernst and our cousin Peter Myers. Ernst and Peter got homesteads northeast of here. Maybe by you, eh?"

Dan shook his head.

"There's some land near ours that nobody's on," he said, "But we haven't any neighbors by the name of Schneider or Myers."

"We file only two weeks ago," John explained. "Ernst and Peter and me built my shanty first because I'm so far away. Then they take wagon and go on to their claims. They go just yesterday. Maybe up your way."

"Are you all farmers?" Dan asked. He hadn't seen any tools about the place but in the snow they could have been obscured.

"No," John told him. "In old country we carpenters. We leave Germany to get out of serving in Kaiser's Army."

"How did you know about homesteads in North Dakota?"

Dan asked. It was hard to believe the news could have spread to Germany.

"We got Uncle in Ann Arbor, Michigan," John explained. "He read about homestead lands and write home to Germany. I just turned twenty-one and Ernst is twenty-two and all we got to do is take out first papers. We tell Peter, then all three come."

Dan understood.

"How are you going to get your land plowed?" he asked.

"Dicker with the neighbors, maybe," John said with a carefree shrug. "I don't know. I find some way. Ernst and Peter and me get claims for . . . what you call it?"

"Speculation?" Dan asked.

"Ya," John nodded. "Come winter, we three go work in logging camp."

Then opening one of the valises, he brought out a zither and began to twang the metallic strings softly.

"You play music?" he asked.

"The guitar, a little," Dan admitted with some satisfaction.

"Music help pass time we got to spend on land," John said, moving his long fingers easily over the strings, and muting carefully with the palm of his left hand. "Ernst play fiddle good. Maybe we get together and make music after I get my acres plowed? Ya?"

Dan was pleased that John accepted him as a musician, and more than pleased that he had found shelter against the storm that continued into the night. The hot stew that John had simmering soon helped to drive the chill from his bones. In the morning, when he peered beyond the canvas door flap, he found clear skies and a warm chinook wind blowing. Soon the snow would be melted and his cold gone too, Dan thought as he tied his scarf about his neck.

"Look up the Osbornes when you come to see Ernst and Peter," he urged as he said good bye to John Schneider.

Relieved of the hobbles and eager to run, Prince made fast work of the few miles between John's shanty and the coulee. It wasn't difficult to find the sheep man's property, for his two-story house and long red barns were visible for many miles. Two tawny shepherd dogs, barking wildly, raced toward Dan as he rode into the yard. They jerked to a sudden halt when they came to the end of the ropes which tied them to a clothes pole, and squarely in his path they continued growling.

Dan sat uncertainly on his horse, for the dogs were far from friendly. As he waited, a thin woman in a grey dress came to the door. She may have said "Hello," but it seemed to Dan that she merely made a small noise.

"I'm looking for a man who has sheep for sale," Dan called to her. "Is this the place?"

She nodded and after a moment pointed to the west. "My man's down in the coulee. Three, four mile, maybe."

"What's his name?" Dan asked.

"Parker. Isaiah Parker." Then to the dogs, "Down, you two! Shut up!"

"Thanks. I'll ride down and see him," Dan said and turned Prince out of the yard.

She stood in the door and watched him ride away, and Dan had an uneasy feeling as he left her and the barking dogs behind. Why weren't the dogs with the sheep? Dan told himself there was sure to be some reasonable explanation. Perhaps those weren't the sheep dogs. All he knew about sheep, after all, had been gleaned from picture books he had read when he was younger than Eddie and Grace.

As Dan rode into the coulee, the b-a-a-a-a-a-ing of the sheep

—64—

came to him with steadily increasing volume. An uninter-
rupted, insistent bleating it seemed and Dan wondered if the
animals kept it up continuously. It would certainly get on a
fellow's nerves, he thought, unless it was possible to get accustomed to it and not hear it at all. Then he heard the sound
of a man's voice, shouting irritably.

"Get out of here! Git, will ye!"

At first no sheep were in sight, then a few rams and ewes
appeared, looking uncertainly up and down the coulee, and
the wind drove an unaccustomed animal smell ahead of them.

The shouts of "Get out!" continued, with curses inter-
mingled, until at last Dan swung around the side of a hill and
into a narrow "U" shaped hollow, to face an unbelievable
sight. Dead and wounded lambs and ewes were piled up against
the narrow bend in the "U", and Isaiah Parker, stick in hand,
was flailing at the uninjured animals in an attempt to drive
them out. Ewes with little lambs were b-a-a-a-aing incessantly,
their cries more like a human wail than an animal's bleat. The
sight of baby lambs, injured and unable to rise, tore at Dan's
heart. Never in his life had he seen a wounded animal before.
What could have caused this sickening horror?

Of his own accord Prince stopped, and Dan sat staring
helplessly at the stomping sheep until at last Mr. Parker saw
him. He straightened up and called to Dan.

"Are you the hand that wuz comin' out?"

Dan shook his head. "No," he managed to say.

"Well, kin you give me a lift?" the man asked. "I've got
to get the ones that ain't hurt outa here."

Dismounting and hobbling Prince, Dan made his way into
the mass of frightened, restless sheep, driving those nearest
him out of the little ravine and into the broader span of the
coulee. For almost an hour he worked, pushing here, shoving

there, until the sweat poured down his back and his senses dulled, and the smell of blood and cries of the animals merged into an unreal background. At last only the wounded remained in the death trap. Mr. Parker stopped then and turned to Dan.

"What happened?" Dan asked.

The wiry, greying man mopped his lean face with a soiled red handkerchief.

"It wuz the storm," he said. "When it came up yesterday, sudden like, some of the ewes wuz lambin' here in the holler. The fool rams came runnin' in for shelter and all the rest follered 'em, stompin' on the ewes that wuz down an' killin' the lambs."

He shoved the handkerchief into the pocket of his faded blue overalls and sighed wearily.

"What about the dogs?" Dan asked, remembering the two animals tied to the clothespole in the Parker yard. "Couldn't they help get them out of here?"

"I tried 'em first off," Mr. Parker explained, rubbing his knotted hands on his soiled clothing. "Then one of 'em got a taste of the blood. A sheep dog's a killer after that. I had to stop and drive the dogs out and tie 'em up, and by that time it wuz dark. Likely I've got to get rid of both of them, too."

Dan understood then why the snarling dogs had been tied. He understood Mrs. Parker's dull, beaten look, too, and could imagine the long night hours that the two of them had spent, helpless against the storm and the unforeseen disaster.

Mr. Parker walked toward the entrance of the hollow and Dan followed him. Against the side of the hill the man had propped his gun and Dan knew well enough what must happen next. The wounded animals would be killed.

—66—

"What wuz you after?" Mr. Parker asked with a suddenness that surprised Dan.

"I . . . well, to tell you the truth I was going to inquire about buying sheep, but right now I don't know," Dan admitted. Right then he was dead certain he didn't want any sheep on the Osborne farm.

"I don't wonder," Mr. Parker agreed. "This wouldn't happen if a feller had barns enough an' kept the ewes in at lambin'. I'll fence off this here coulee so they don't get in here again."

He wiped the gun barrel with the handkerchief that a few moments before had cleared the perspiration from his deeply lined face.

"I dunno . . ." he continued after a pause. "I dunno if I've got any to sell now. 'Pears to me I gotta either sell 'em all or keep 'em all, now. I ain't certain how many I got to sell."

"I guess I ought to talk to my brother before I decide, anyway," Dan said. "I was going on to Williston to get in touch with him."

"What's his name?" Mr. Parker asked, looking off toward the coulee hills.

"Osborne," Dan replied. "Charles Osborne, Jr. 'Slim' he's usually called."

"Yeah?" Mr. Parker said slowly and it seemed to Dan that he was suddenly cautious and withdrawing. Then: "Whatta I owe you?"

"You don't owe me anything," Dan answered. "With a loss like this it was little enough a fellow could do for you."

"Don't make it out worse'n it is," Mr. Parker said. "I ain't wiped out. Just a few lambs. You allus lose a few."

He was trying to make light of the loss now. Why, Dan wondered. Had the Interests financed his sheep business, too?

Whatever the reason, Dan wanted only to get away from the horrible sight and the sickening sounds and smells.

It was like wakening from a nightmare to gallop out of the coulee onto the open prairie where the wind was fresh and the snow was melting. Prairie chickens rose ahead of his path in low, sputtering flight. Meadow larks whistled clearly, cheerfully. This was the land Dan loved, this great flat table-land that he could turn into rich, black fields. Fields that soon would wave with grain. He could picture his own acres greening, growing, turning gold, come August.

"Wheat country, Prince," Dan said to his horse. "That's what this is. And I don't want any sheep. I can't help what Mom wants. All I want is . . ."

But he didn't say it aloud, even to Prince.

Ahead of him the Missouri glistened in the sun. The "Big Muddy" that had brought the first settlers to Williston before Jim Hill's railroad reached the town with its round house and repair shops. He could see the towering grain elevators now and the houses and stores clustering at their feet. On a terrace the town seemed to lie, between the lowlands of the tree-lined Missouri and the rolling hills and prairie. He'd be there before night. He'd ask the question again: "Charles Osborne, Jr. 'Slim' they usually call him. Do you know him?"

And somebody would answer "Yes."

6. *Slim Osborne*

THE first man Dan questioned knew Slim; knew where he could be located, too. Dan hurried along the main street of Williston in the after-glow of the sunset to a restaurant near the depot. He had been hungry as he rode the last miles into town, but it was nervousness and not hunger that knotted his stomach while he hesitated at the restaurant door. He'd been rehearsing what he'd say to Slim for days; how he'd tell him about Gramps and Pa; how he'd ask him to come home. Now he didn't know what he'd say. But he couldn't stand there outside the place all night. Deliberately he pushed the door open and walked in.

The sign said "Restaurant" and the man who had told him where he would find Slim had called the place a restaurant, but it wasn't what Dan had expected to see. Along one side of the dining room there was a long, bare bar with bottles in neat rows against a mirror behind the counter. Beyond the bar there was another room which Dan could just glimpse, and in the doorway leading to it, relaxed and lazy-like, stood Slim.

There wasn't any mistaking him, although his back was turned to Dan. A light blue store shirt and tight-fitting black trousers seemed to call attention to his tall, bony frame and the bowed left knee. Leaning against the door jamb he was plainly at home in this strange place, heavy with the smells of tobacco smoke and liquor and frying food.

Dan sat down at an empty table near the door. Somehow he couldn't go right up to Slim. Not in front of all the men in the place, not knowing what Slim would do. He'd wait a bit. Maybe let Slim see him first.

Dan looked about the room. Kerosene lamps, flickering against bright reflectors, hung on all four walls. One stoop-shouldered waiter, white apron tucked in the top of his trousers, shuffled about with plates of food. The tables were bare and bare too was the rough board floor, stained with dirt and tobacco juice. Clattering dishes, scraping chairs, and the shuffling steps of the waiter were a half-heard background of sound as Dan watched his brother, his own heart thumping hard inside him.

"What'll it be?"

Dan heard the waiter all right, but he hadn't considered what he would eat. He didn't answer right away. He was trying to collect his thoughts.

"I say, Red, what'll it be?"

The demand was loud and somewhat gruff, and Slim turned to glance over his shoulder into the dining room. Dan saw him start, saw the look of surprise in his dark eyes. Then slowly, tantalizingly it seemed to Dan, Slim came toward him. There was a trace of a smile about his lips but it wasn't a smile of welcome. Unconsciously Dan braced himself.

"Well, Red, how are you?" Slim asked. "Duffy here wants to know what you'll have."

The smile still lifted Slim's moustached lip but there was no smile in his eyes. He slipped his fingers inside his trouser belt and looked down at Dan with a needling, irritating self-confidence. Dan felt his temper rising. He mustn't let Slim see that. He was glad the wind and sun had toughened his skin so the flush of anger wouldn't show. Deliberately he turned from Slim to the waiter.

"Ham and eggs and a cup of coffee," he said, then gestured to the empty chair opposite him.

Slim pulled the chair back from the table and sat down.

"Bring me some coffee, will you, Duffy?" he asked.

"Sure thing," the waiter said and after a moment's hesitation shuffled off.

Slim tilted his chair back and linked his fingers behind his neck. For a few moments he looked at Dan without speaking, then he settled the chair back on the floor and began to roll a cigarette.

"I figured you'd make Williston sooner or later," he said. "I've been expecting you."

Dan watched as Slim pulled the tobacco bag shut and lit a match. Slim hadn't smoked when he left home. But this wasn't the Slim who had run away. Or was it? Slim had been bitter those last few months at home when he'd worked around the depot shoving baggage. He'd given most of the money he'd earned to Mom, to help with expenses at home. There'd been little enough left for himself at the end of the week and no hope of a better job, Dan remembered. Now he was expecting the family to ask for help again. That was what was bothering him, all right. That and something else that Dan wanted to know more about. "Everything's wrong," Slim had said back in Minot. The memory of that stormy night, of Slim's worried face, quieted Dan's sudden anger. He hadn't come to Williston to make things worse for Slim.

"I'd have looked you up before, only I had to get the crops in first," Dan said and was surprised at the evenness of his own voice. "There's things you don't know, Slim."

"Like what?"

"That Gramps died, for one thing."

The news didn't seem to affect his brother very much, one way or another. Dan knew he'd have to tell more, but Slim wasn't making it easy for him to go on. He wasn't asking any questions or showing any interest.

"Gramps had some money, Slim," Dan finally blurted out. "A lot more than Mom ever knew. We aren't in debt to the Interests like you think. We've paid for everything."

The half-burned cigarette almost fell from Slim's fingers and the hard look on his face changed for a moment. Dan watched him anxiously. If Slim would only ask a question . . . make one friendly gesture. But instead he threw the cigarette on the floor and getting up, stepped on it deliberately.

"Well, that's a relief," he said and walked to the bar.

There didn't seem to be anything more Dan could say or do. And there was so much he wanted to tell Slim. Well, he wouldn't go trailing to the bar after him. It was Slim's next move. When the waiter brought his food, Dan began to eat it and as he ate the tension eased. He'd managed to get part of the story to Slim, anyway. If Slim didn't come back to the table he'd just go over and say good bye and see whether Slim would give him another chance.

But Slim came back. He sat down and pushed aside the cup of coffee Duffy had left for him.

"What's on your mind, Red?" he asked looking intently at Dan. "Why did you look me up?"

"Because of Pa and Mom and the kids," Dan replied. "They want to know where you are. How you are."

"Did they send you? Just for that reason?"

"No," Dan admitted. "There was business, too."

Dan knew he must be cautious now. He couldn't let Slim know that Pa and Mom never mentioned his name. He mustn't spoil this opening Slim was giving him.

"What business?"

The question was direct and honest. This was more like Slim.

"We haven't bought our haying machines nor our harvester," Dan told him. "Mom figured we might do better in Williston than in Minot. Then if we buy sheep, we've got to get fencing, too."

"Buy sheep?" Slim asked and a frown clouded his face. "You aren't going to buy sheep?"

"I don't know. Why not?"

"Look, Red, I've no right to be telling you what to do. I can see that," Slim said. "But I am telling you not to take sheep into grain country."

"One man's done it," Dan said slowly. "We've got land we couldn't get into crops this year. What's wrong with putting sheep on it and making money off it? It's a loss as it stands."

"All I'm saying is, don't take sheep into grain country," Slim repeated. "And if you're referring to Isaiah Parker, he's trying to sell his sheep, right now."

Dan was about to ask for what reason when he recalled Isaiah Parker's final request: "Don't make it out no worse than it is." There was something back of all this. He must keep Slim talking if he could.

"You've been here longer than us, Slim," Dan said. "You probably know. We haven't bought any sheep yet, but I saw Parker on the way to Williston."

"Let him get rid of his sheep some other way," Slim said and rolled another cigarette.

"All right, but why?" Dan asked.

Slim looked around the room before answering and Dan's eyes followed his from table to table. Rough looking men these were. Not farmers surely, nor the merchants of the town. Railroad men, perhaps, who worked in the Great Northern shops? Men who worked for the Interests? Dan looked at his brother again.

"What about sheep?" he asked.

Slim scowled. "Who do you figure opened up this section of the country, Red?" he asked. Then without waiting for a reply he answered his own question. "The Great Northern Railroad. And why? Because they figure it's rich grain country. They've brought settlers here to farm the land. They've built elevators. They've got cars to take the stuff to the mills in Minneapolis. They've set men up in business to sell everything from sugar to plows. All because of wheat. The cattle men and the sheep men have got to stay on the Missouri slope and down toward the Badlands. Let them fight it out there."

Slim's face was dark and tense as he said it. It was clear enough that he was on the side of the Railroad and against a man like Isaiah Parker who wanted to raise sheep instead of grain.

"Parker's got to sell his sheep then?" Dan asked, wondering as he questioned his brother why the man had not tried harder to sell them to him.

Slim nodded. "Sell them or move them out." Then after a pause, "If you aren't in debt to the Interests, don't get in debt. And don't try to buck them, either."

"If buying sheep is bucking them I don't think I'll be doing it," Dan said. Then, before he thought he added, "I didn't like what I saw of the sheep business."

"What do you mean?"

Slim was alert, leaning forward a little now, looking at Dan intently. Once more Isaiah Parker's wariness came back to Dan's memory. It was when Dan had said he was going to Williston that Mr. Parker suddenly had been on guard. Slowly things were beginning to take shape. Mr. Parker was just one individual who had wanted to raise sheep, but here in Williston there were representatives of the Interests who wanted the settlers to raise grain . . . farm with the machines and tools they'd brought in . . . take the grain to their elevators . . . ship it in their cars to their mills in Minneapolis. They could run a man like Isaiah Parker, and his beaten-looking wife, out of business. Could and would, and somehow Slim was involved with them.

"What did you see?"

It was Slim, pressing for information, his dark eyes eager and his look penetrating.

Dan knew he'd have to answer, but if he told Slim what he'd seen he would be dooming Isaiah Parker in some way. He was sure of it.

Dan wrinkled his nose. "It was the ewes a-lambing, I guess," he said. "The bleatings and the smells and all. I'd rather raise grain."

He avoided Slim's eyes and inside he shuddered as he waited to see whether the answer satisfied Slim. Why had Slim gotten tied up with the Interests and how? Perhaps he might as well ask outright. Perhaps the question would take Slim's mind off the sheep.

"Slim, what are you doing? To earn a living, I mean."

Slim leaned back in his chair, his arms across his chest. Clearly he had anticipated that question too, just as he had expected Dan's visit.

"Odd jobs," he answered with a slight shrug. "Right now, watching over this," and with a jerk of his head he indicated the room back of the bar.

"Gambling?" Dan asked.

Slim nodded. "You'd better not describe it in detail to Mom," he said.

It was the first time Slim had mentioned Mom. He hadn't even asked about her or Pa or the kids. Didn't he want to know about them? He must!

"She'd awfully like to see you," Dan said quietly. But that was all he could say. He was afraid now to tell Slim about Pa. Would Slim think he must tell the Interests that Pa couldn't work the land? Dan forced the thought out of his mind. Slim wouldn't do that. Probably the Interests already knew that the Osbornes had less than 80 acres in, and couldn't make any money this year. Cautiously Dan glanced at his brother, waiting for Slim to answer, but Slim stared blankly at the bar, his features set and grim. He wasn't responding to the invitation. He wasn't going to. More than anything in the world Dan wanted Slim to come home. They needed him, Mom and Pa. Dan needed him, but slowly it became clear that Dan and Mom would have to manage without him, just as Mom had said.

Dan pushed his chair back from the table. He might as well end the conversation and go. He still had to find a place to spend the night. As he stood up Slim rose too, and faced Dan across the table. Tall as Slim was, Dan noted with pride that he had grown almost to Slim's height. It gave him confidence, and across the table he looked Slim squarely in the eye. And as he stood there, suddenly he was mad. Thoroughly mad at Slim.

"You're tied in with the Interests, aren't you?" Dan demanded. "This . . ." and he looked about the room, "This is just a . . ." he paused for lack of a word.

"A front? Is that what you're trying to say?" Slim asked.

In a way it was what Dan meant, but he ignored Slim and went on bitterly.

"You don't care anything about any of us, do you? Pa or Mom or even the kids!"

With a suddenness that took Dan's breath away Slim grabbed his arm and swung him around so they faced each other with no table separating them. Slim's face had gone white and his mouth and eyes were hard.

"I care enough to ask one great big favor of you, Red," he said hoarsely. "Just don't tell them you saw me, hear?"

"I hear," Dan said jerking his arm free. "You don't think I'd tell them anything like this? I'd be ashamed to!"

"What about Minot?" Slim's voice was almost a whisper.

"I didn't tell them I saw you there either," Dan answered. "And for the same reason!"

"Okay," Slim said. "Leave it that way."

Then he turned from the table and walked out of the restaurant, slamming the door behind him.

Dan was conscious now of watching eyes, and men who had stopped eating. He took his cap from the back of his chair and reached in his pocket for money. He'd pay for his food and go. As he looked for the waiter the man came slowly toward him.

"I ain't never seen you here before, have I?" he asked and waited.

"No and you aren't likely to see me again," Dan answered pushing a silver dollar into the outstretched, hollow hand. The man fumbled in his pocket and brought out a handful of silver. Carefully he counted the change.

"That Slim Osborne ain't no man to tangle with," he said cautiously.

"Neither am I," Dan answered gruffly. "He doesn't own this place, does he?"

"No, but the one who does draws a lot of water."

Dan turned away without answering. He didn't care who owned the place or who Slim worked for. Apparently Slim had the decency to be ashamed, but if he was why did he stay there?

Outside the chill air cleared Dan's head and he hurried back to the livery stable where he had left Prince. He'd ask the man about a place to sleep. Perhaps he could curl up in his blankets in the hay loft. If there wasn't anyone about, that was what he intended to do. He couldn't be wasting money on hotel rooms.

The barn door was ajar and Dan stepped quietly inside. Shadows flickered in the lantern light as horses switched their tails and moved about. There was a good smell in the place; the smell of hay and oats and fresh straw and healthy animals.

Dan started toward the ladder leading to the loft, then he saw a figure moving cautiously from one of the empty stalls.

"Dan, is that you?"

Dan stopped in his tracks. At first he couldn't recognize the voice that cautiously whispered his name. Then he knew.

"Tom! Tom Sheets, what are you doing here?"

"Looking for you," Tom whispered. "I found Prince, so I knew you'd be along. Your Maw had word she wanted to get to you, so I up and followed you."

7. Politics

FOR a moment, Dan stared at Tom, scarcely comprehending the meaning of his words. Then fear panicked him.

"Pa?"

His lips were dry and he could scarcely whisper the word. If Mom had sent for him he could think of but one reason. Pa must have been taken worse.

At first Tom didn't understand Dan's question, but when he did he quickly answered "No." Then Dan could breathe again.

"What's up?" he asked in a guarded whisper.

"They're holding an election," Tom replied. "Your Maw was afraid you wouldn't get back in time to get your old man to it."

"Is that all?" Dan asked.

"Yeah," Tom said. "I didn't think it was so all-fired important but she was awful riled up about it, some way. Wants you to get right back home."

If Mom was so disturbed that she would send Tom Sheets after him, Dan was sure there must be something to it. For all Mom knew, Dan might be bargaining for sheep, and against Ike Sheets' advice. But now was no time to be talking about it.

Dan took the saddle blankets from the side of Prince's stall and tiptoed to the ladder leading to the loft, Tom close behind him.

The supply of fodder at the livery stable clearly had dwindled in the months since last haying season, and cautiously Dan felt his way across the mow, guided by a ribbon of moonlight that streamed through one small window. Floor boards creaked brashly and a cricket set up a noisy protest at the intrusion. It was enough to arouse all Williston. When at last Dan found a mound of hay in the far corner of the loft, he passed a blanket to Tom and the two rolled up, side by side, on their dry and dusty bed.

Tom was sleeping in a few minutes but Dan lay, wide-eyed, his thoughts on Slim. The rough blanket scratched his neck and he tossed it back irritably. Again he saw the restaurant . . . the dim light and heavy smells . . . the podgy old waiter . . . the gambling room . . . Slim walking toward him, his thin lips smiling and his eyes so cold . . . Then Slim seemed to be riding away on Prince, but not toward home . . .

Dan awakened to find the loft window framing a rose-colored mist and could scarcely believe he had been asleep and that the night was gone. He poked at Tom and in another minute the two were leading their horses out of the livery stable.

"Wonder if there'll be a restaurant open," Tom whispered, his teeth chattering in the chill of the morning. "I ain't had anything to eat since yesterday noon when I finished up the sandwiches your Maw give me."

"Why didn't you say so last night?" Dan asked. "Mom should have given you enough to last till you got here. I'm surprised she didn't."

"Oh, she give me enough all right," Tom hastened to assure him. "Swell grub, too. Chicken sandwiches and hard boiled eggs and cake. I just got awful hungry riding, and et it all."

Dan glanced at Tom as he jumped easily onto his horse. Meals at the Sheets shanty he could well believe were meager and tasteless. No wonder Tom was fairly skin and bones. But he was riding with a skill that Dan had not attained, moving gracefully with his unsaddled horse and slapping its shoulders gently. There was a look of satisfaction about him too, as though he was pleased to be riding through Williston with Dan. If only his scraggly hair had been cut, Dan wouldn't need to be ashamed of him. Not even if he met Slim. Dan told himself he didn't want to see Slim again, and the thought of another encounter did indeed send a chill through him, yet he hated to leave Williston like this. It was worse than not seeing Slim at all.

Dan had no intention of going for breakfast to the restaurant where he had met his brother the night before, although he was sure Slim would not be there at this hour. Only a few men were on the street, and following in the direction they were going he soon came to a tar-paper-covered shack with a small sign that read "Cafe."

"Wisht there was some place to clean up," Tom said as he slid from his horse and tied it to the hitching post. Once again Dan glanced at him. Certainly Tom was trying to shed the

Sheets habits and be more like the Osbornes and the Nelsons, for this trip at least.

Pancakes, sausage and hot coffee were a good enough start for any day. With a bag of sandwiches and doughnuts to tide them over until night, when they should reach a half-way house, Dan and Tom started out onto the prairie and toward home.

"You're sure Mom was anxious for me to come right back?" Dan questioned. "I'd intended to see about buying haying machinery. It seems crazy to start back without getting anything done."

"She said there's no real hurry about what you're doing," Tom assured him. "You can go again before haying time, she said, but the election's been called and it won't be put off."

"When is it?" Dan asked.

"Tomorrow night," Tom answered and digging his knees into the horse's side he moved a little ahead of Dan.

"Tomorrow night?" Dan repeated. "How could that be? Isn't that awful short notice?"

Tom, still riding ahead, did not answer, so Dan gave Prince a slap and easily pulled up beside him.

"How come?" Dan pressed.

"Well," Tom hesitated, "the election was actually called a couple-a weeks ago. Mebee longer. Nobody told your Paw because . . . well, you know . . . My old man thought it might make him feel bad, beings as how he likely wouldn't want to go."

Tom's old man! Was it Ike Sheets who had called the election? Dan hated to ask outright, but he wanted to know.

"I didn't hear anything about it," Dan said. "How did Mom find out?"

"I guess Chris or Nels told her," Tom said evasively. "I'd

of said something to you but I never happened to see you after it was called. It didn't seem so important."

"It sure seems funny to me that Mom would ask you to come all the way to Williston unless it was important," Dan said. "Why did she do it?"

"She didn't exactly ask me," Tom admitted. "I was down at your place watering my horse after Paw rode off to Minot and she asked me where Paw got the information about calling it. I could see she was getting more and more worked up, so I said I'd just as lief ride to Williston and get you to come home. I didn't have nothing much to do."

Dan nodded. So Ike Sheets had called the election and hadn't let the Osbornes know about it. Probably Jim Jackson and the Nelsons thought Ike had told Mom, and hadn't said anything about it on account of Pa being as he was.

They rode in silence after that. The sky was cloudless and blue above them. Prairie plover called across the endless plains and gophers scampered away at the sound of the horses' hooves. Dan's mind went back to Williston and Slim. Somehow, he should have let Slim know about Pa. Now it looked as though Slim never would come home and he didn't know why, for a certainty.

How were the unbroken acres on the Osborne homestead to be plowed this season and seeded next spring. There was hay to be cut and stacked for winter too, and harvesting to be done. The barn wasn't up nor the grainery built. How was he to get it done all alone? He thought of Jim Jackson and the possibility that John and Ernst Schneider might lend a hand, if they had really settled in the neighborhood.

"Say, Tom, you haven't heard of a couple of Germans taking up claims out our way, have you?" Dan asked. "I met a fellow by the name of John Schneider and he said his brother and cousin had land in our direction."

"Yeah," Tom replied. "They're just across from the Nelsons. Paw run into 'em last time he was in Minot but they only got out onto their claims this week. Came in night before the storm and bunked with us."

Two more settlers in the county meant two more votes in this election, Dan realized. Mom would have known about that too, likely enough. There was something up, all right. Ike was the only man these Germans knew. If Ike had any schemes afoot doubtless he could count on the newcomers to vote his way. Dan was sure now that his mother had good reason for sending Tom to bring him home. Tom was the only one she could send. The Nelson boys had work to do and she couldn't ask them to leave it to run an errand for her.

"Come on," Dan said giving Prince a resounding slap. "Let's get going."

It was increasingly clear as they neared home the next day that Tom was anxious to be there ahead of his father. He leaned over his horse, straining his eyes to see his own shanty. When at last it came within view he said with obvious relief, "He ain't home yet."

How tiny the shanty looked. Even Dan's own two-story house beside the willows was like an overturned box on a desert that the wind could toss about like a tumble weed. Those half-dozen buildings that comprised Dan's world had never seemed so small before, nor the prairie so vast, nor the task of turning it into farm land so impossible. Nor had Dan ever felt more disconsolate than when he rode into his own yard and to the trough at the well.

Mom and Eddie and Grace had been working in the garden. The children, shouting to their dog, ran to meet him with

Mom close on their heels. Their hands were dirty, their faces sweaty, and as Mom straightened herself Dan saw that she looked tired and that her hair was more gray than he had realized. Once more he felt a surge of anger as he thought of Slim. How could Slim refuse to help them when they needed him so badly? Or was it Dan's own fault that Slim hadn't come home?

"Tom, it was right good of you to get Dan back in time," Mom was saying. "Come on in and have a bite to eat. You must both be tired and hungry."

"I'd better get on home and put the beans on," Tom said. "I can expect my old man any time now."

Mom didn't urge Tom to stay. She gave him a loaf of freshly-baked bread and as soon as he was gone she turned to Dan.

"I hated to send for you before you'd had a chance to do anything, but Pa's got to be at that election tonight," she explained. "How much did Tom tell you?"

"Just that there's to be one, and no one let us know about it," Dan answered. "What's likely to happen?"

"Unless I miss my guess, Ike Sheets has everything all schemed out," Mom said. "There's just one thing I'm anxious about, and that's who gets to be county school commissioner. If Ike gets himself named school commissioner, or one of these bachelors who've just come onto their claims, we'll have no school this year, or next either likely enough. And Eddie's got to go to school, Dan. You know that."

Dan looked about the kitchen. Eddie and Grace had remained outside so Dan was free to talk.

"Does it seem to you that Eddie imagines a lot of things, Mom?" Dan asked. "He tells me stuff and I never know whether it's the truth or something he dreamed up."

"Eddie's like your Pa, Dan." Mom confided. "Call it imagination or what you will. He's got more of a mind than Grace. She's like me. She'll get along with little or no schooling, but Eddie . . ." She sighed and left the sentence unfinished.

"I know what you mean, Mom," Dan said. "He's got to have a better chance. That's what we came out here for."

"What did you find out about the sheep, Dan? Anything?" Mom asked, interrupting his thoughts.

Dan had decided on the ride home what he would tell her. He enlarged on Isaiah Parker's troubles and his dread of the Interests.

"I didn't have any time in Williston as you know," he finished. "I'd just eaten my supper and gone back to the livery stable when I found Tom waiting for me. But I got to talking with men at the restaurant. There's some sort of feud going on between the grain Interests and the sheep and cattle men. Isaiah Parker's got to sell out, but the Interests want him to take his sheep back into the Badlands section to the southwest and out of the grain country."

Dan didn't look at his mother as he told the story. It would be difficult to look into those green eyes and hide his secret. But Mom knew he'd had no time in Williston. She seemed to believe he'd told her everything.

"If sheep are out of the question, then we've got to get the rest of the land broke this summer and fall, ready to seed next spring," Mom said when he had finished. "I don't know how we're going to do it exactly, but it's clear enough we've got to get income off every acre next year."

Dan nodded but he didn't know how they were going to do it either.

"Right now the worry is how to get Mr. Nelson elected school commissioner," Mom went on. "If I'd known about this election in time, I'd have done some campaigning too. Now all we can do is make sure Pa gets his name up. Folks like Mr. Nelson. Maybe he can carry it, against whoever Ike Sheets put up."

"I suppose Ike would be against schools, just on general principles," Dan said.

"Not general principles," Mom explained. "Taxes. There has to be money to build a school and hire a teacher, Dan. There's a state school fund but it doesn't allow much for a district with less than fifteen children, and there aren't fifteen children in this end of the county as you well know."

"Gosh, Mom, where are we going to get money for school taxes?" Dan protested. "Money! That seems to be the most important thing in the world!"

"It wouldn't be so much," his mother assured him. "Anyhow, Dan, there's got to be a school whether we have anything else or not. So you get yourself cleaned up and ready."

Dan never forgot that night.

The first election in the county was held in the Nelsons' barn. While the women sat in the house and visited, the men gathered in the twilight outside their designated meeting place. Nels and Chris helped Dan get Pa's wheel chair out of the wagon and inside the building. The days were long now. Twelve hours of sunshine, and by June there would be sixteen hours, but as soon as the sun dropped below the horizon there was a chill night air that wasn't good for Pa.

It pleased Dan to see all of the neighbors come up and speak to Pa. Mom had shaved him and cut his hair, and he and Dan were both dressed in their store suits. Pa had an air about him all right, even in his wheel chair, and he said "Good evening," and "Fine weather," as plain as anyone. He even asked Jim Jackson about his garden, and while Jim didn't quite understand the question Mr. Nelson spoke up and the conversation went right on with Pa taking part almost like the rest of the men. Even the strangers from the far side of the county acted friendly and nodded to him when he smiled at them.

Ike Sheets was the last to arrive. He didn't have any good clothes to wear for the occasion, but he'd had his hair cut in Minot and he was shaved, and he looked better than Dan had ever seen him look before. He had two strangers with him, and Dan was sure they were Ernst Schneider and Peter Myers. Waiting beside his father, Dan wondered what Ike would say when he finally got to them, for he was shaking hands all around.

If Ike was surprised to see Pa there, he didn't show it. He shook hands with Pa too.

"These here are our newest neighbors," he said as he introduced the Germans.

"I met your brother John earlier this week," Dan said as he shook Ernst Schneider's hand. "He's coming up one of these days with his zither, and we're going to try a little music together."

"Music?"

Ernst and Peter were interested at once, and Dan determined to keep them with him and Pa. Ernst was shorter than his brother, and both he and Peter were fair skinned and blonde, but neither was handsome like John. They were much more like each other, Dan saw. Round features and full lips and large, strong bodies.

"Mom has an organ and I've got a guitar," Dan told his new friends. "I can't play like John, of course. He's a real musician. And he says you're some fiddler, Ernst."

Ernst was pleased. He found a seat on a half-finished stall

beside Pa and motioned Peter to sit beside him. This wasn't what Ike had wanted, but Ernst and Peter didn't sense it. They questioned Dan about his visit with John and laughed as he told them of stumbling onto John's shack in the blizzard.

Mr. Nelson finally called the meeting to order by welcoming everyone to his place. Before he had fairly finished talking, Jim Jackson was on his feet and nominated Ike Sheets as chairman of the meeting.

Dan hadn't expected it. The suddenness of the nomination brought him back to the importance of the business they had come for. Mom had said Ike probably had everything schemed out, and it looked as though she was right. One of the men from across the county shouted "second the nomination" and Jim said "All in favor say 'aye'" and before Dan rightly sensed what was happening Ike was in charge of the meeting.

Dan glanced at Jim questioningly but Jim wasn't looking at him. Well enough Dan remembered that Jim once had said he wouldn't like Ike for an enemy. He was bidding now to keep Ike as a friend.

With a wave of the hand Ike accepted the nomination and walked to the center of the barn floor. He was pleased all right.

"I've been to Minot a couple-a times this spring and I asked some friends of mine how we should go about organizin'," he began. "I got it from the fellers there who know, so can pass it on to you. Primaries is held in June and elections is held in November of the even years, so this is an election year. It ain't June yet, so what we should do is elect temporary commissioners tonight. If this county wants a primary next month, the commissioners can go ahead and call one. That's what I'm told on good authority."

Ike stopped after his speech and looked about the room. No one questioned him so he continued.

"What we're here for tonight is to elect three county commissioners, one for three years, one for two years, and one for one year. They can meet and transact business for the county. Do I hear any nominations?"

Dan didn't know the man who nominated Ike for commissioner for three years, nor the man who seconded the nomination. They came from across the county. He was still looking over the crowd and wondering what would happen next when he heard Ike saying "All in favor say 'aye'" and Ike was elected.

Then Ernst Schneider nominated Jim Jackson for the two-year office and Ike was calling for a nomination for commissioner for one year while Dan was still wondering how Ernst even knew Jim. It was all happening so fast Dan couldn't keep up with it. Somebody nominated Mr. Nelson and then Pa spoke out, good and clear too.

"Mister Chairman!"

Ike looked at Pa in surprise.

"What is it, Osborne?" he asked and scowled a little as he said it.

"Can . . . one . . . com-m-m . . ."

Pa couldn't get the word out and Dan didn't know what he was trying to say. He felt his hands getting wet with sweat and his collar was choking him. And Pa kept trying to get the sentence said.

". . . one . . . hold . . . two . . ."

Then Dan thought he understood. He leaned over his father and whispered the question: "Can one commissioner hold two offices? Is that what you mean?"

Pa wiped his perspiring forehead and nodded.

"Mr. Chairman," Dan said and his voice shook but he knew he could ask the question. "Pa wants to ask if one commissioner can hold two offices."

Ike scratched his head.

"I don't know if questions is in order during voting or not," Ike said, "But anyway, I'd say no. One man can't hold two offices."

Pa took a firm grip on Dan's arm then and made one more attempt to speak.

"I . . . wish . . . to propose . . . Mr. Nelson for . . . school . . . com-m-m—"

It wasn't very intelligible. Dan knew what Pa was trying to say but his voice had dropped and very few other people understood. Everyone was looking at them, and now Ike Sheets was plainly irritated. Dan knew he would have to speak for Pa again, and he was afraid Pa was out of order.

"He says he wants to propose Mr. Nelson for school commissioner," Dan said.

"We ain't votin' on school commissioner," Ike announced. "Like I said in the beginnin', this here is just a meetin' to get organized. School commissioners is elected in November. If we want a primary in June to nominate 'em, the commissioners we elect now can call one. I got it right from the fellers who runs Minot."

Dan held his breath. He didn't see how Pa could get Mr. Nelson nominated for school commissioner, to say nothing of electing him. Nobody was protesting the way Ike was running the meeting. Pa was the only one who knew how to protest, and he couldn't get the words out clearly enough.

"Now if there's no more questions, we'll vote on Mr. Nelson as county commissioner for one year," Ike announced.

Mr. Nelson was elected and then Ike called for a motion

to adjourn, and in fifteen minutes it was all over. There hadn't been a chance to even talk about getting a school started. There hadn't been a thing Pa could do. Ike was commissioner for three years and Jim for two years and if they decided not to hold a primary in June there was nothing Mr. Nelson could do or anyone else, Dan was sure. He leaned over his father again.

"Was there anything I could have done, Pa?" he whispered.

Pa shook his head. With his good right hand he started wheeling his chair toward the door. Then Mr. Nelson came over to him.

"This was a surprise," he said in a low voice. "I didn't know. Nobody said anything to me. I think it was . . . how do you say it?"

"Fixed," Pa answered. "Cut . . . and . . . dried." He said it in a voice loud enough so Ike Sheets and Jim Jackson could hear, too.

Dan pushed the wheel chair out of the barn quickly. He had trouble enough without ill will over the election results, and that's what there would be if Pa said any more. Dan had been counting on Jim Jackson and maybe Ernst and Peter to help him with the work he couldn't do alone. Now they were all over on the other side of the barn, shaking hands with Ike Sheets. Why, oh why had Pa and Mom had to get mixed up in politics? He had to have help from someone. Who could he turn to now?

8. Red Night

IKE and Tom Sheets gave Jim Jackson a hand as he dug his well and started work on his barn. Across the flat acres that separated the homesteads Dan could see them plainly. Jim had avoided the Osbornes since the night he had helped get Ike elected county commissioner and Dan felt miserable about it. Jim shouldn't act that way. Dan could understand that Jim had to nominate Ike if the favor was asked of him. Especially if Ike had promised to get Jim elected to office in return. But it had created a division in the neighborhood and Dan didn't know what to do about it.

As for Tom, Dan hadn't expected to see much of him until Ike made another of his trips to Minot. Tom never failed to be solidly with his father, so long as Ike was around, at least.

To the south the Nelsons were hammering from dawn until dark, erecting barns, building a guard around their new well, and watering troughs for their animals. And with wells of their own at last, there was no need for the neighbors to gather each night at the Osborne place, so Dan was very much alone.

It was slow business, too, trying to get a barn up with no one to help except Mom. First of all the lumber had to be hauled from the knoll near the house where it had been unloaded to the barn site Pa had pointed out.

"Drainage," Pa had said and after a few questions and patient listening, Dan had understood. The barns must drain away from the well.

"We've got to take more time with Pa," Mom said between puffs and gasps as she tugged at the heavy planks. "We've got to get him talking by June."

Dan shoved the plank into place. "June?" he asked.

"There's going to be a primary election in June and he's got to be put up for school commissioner," Mom explained. "The voting's going to be done right here in this barn."

Dan dropped the two-by-four he was holding with a heavy thud. "Oh, Mom!" he groaned.

But Mom's chin was set and her voice almost gravelly as she answered him.

"Ike Sheets isn't going to keep us from having a school," she said. "He isn't going to stop me this time."

"But Mom," Dan protested. "You know what happened last time. The neighbors aren't speaking to us any more."

"Now Dan, that's not so," Mom contradicted. "Just because they've got their wells dug at last, and are too busy to come a-visiting, isn't any sign the neighbors are against us. Now get that two-by-four up!"

Dan set the beam in place and pounded hard at the spikes while Mom held it for him.

"Furthermore, we're going to start a school here too," Mom announced. "Soon as we get the barn roof up!"

"A school in our barn," Dan scoffed. "Who's going to teach it—Pa?"

"Yes," came the quick retort. "He's got an education. He's the only man in the county who's ever been to college."

Dan stopped work to stare at his mother in amazement. What was she thinking of?

"Now don't stand there with your mouth open," Mom almost snapped. "There'll be no school unless we do something and I know what we're going to do."

"Well what?" Dan demanded. "And how?"

"Now this is just between you and me, Dan," Mom said lowering her voice. "I wrote to the Agriculture College at Fargo about it, weeks ago. They sent my letter to the state superintendent of education in Bismarck and he wrote back. Ike Sheets brought me the letter when he came from Minot last time, not knowing what was in it, of course. So I know the school law better than he does and I'm on to his tricks now, too."

Dan ran his hands through his touseled red hair in dismay. If Mom was going to keep on stirring up politics he could see nothing but trouble ahead.

"Mom, what are you figuring on doing?" he asked cautiously.

"First off I'm going to let every family know that Pa'll teach school this summer at no cost to anybody. Then when the primary comes up, I'm going to get his name put up for school commissioner. Folks will think that if he can teach he can hold office too. And with the practice he'll get talking to the kids, he can be commissioner by the time the election comes up in November. That way we'll get a school."

She had it all thought out, Dan could see.

"Who's going to help you with all this politics?" Dan asked. If Mom thought he was going to run around the county like Ike Sheets had done, getting votes lined up in advance, he'd certainly have to begin thinking of some way out, right away.

But Mom had a different idea. "Petra's going to help," she announced.

"Petra?" Dan couldn't see how.

"Right off she's just going to get word around about the school," Mom explained. "She's going to all the families in the county. I told her she could ride Prince."

"That would do it," Dan agreed and in spite of himself he almost smiled. "She's been wanting to ride Prince ever since the night she caught him."

"And now she's going to," Mom said with finality.

But Dan himself rode Prince, and on a bitter journey, before the day when Petra spread the news about the school. That very night he was wakened by Punkin jumping on his bed, then rushing to the window whining and growling. He was about to slide back under the blankets when the dog jumped on him again, whining low. Something was wrong, Dan knew. Cautiously he got out of bed and followed the pup to the window. At first he could not see anything for there was no moon, but as Punkin's sniffs and growls continued, and Dan peered in the direction of the unfinished barn, he at last could see horses moving.

Horse thieves! He knew it in an instant and was wide awake. Grabbing for trousers and shoes he hurried downstairs to the room where his father was sleeping. The shot gun was there. He hadn't intended to waken Pa, but as he tiptoed into the room his father spoke.

"Someone . . . at the . . . horses?" he whispered.

"Yes. I'll try to drive them off."

"Shoot . . . high," Pa cautioned. "Don't . . . try to . . . hit."

It was good advice, Dan realized. He didn't want to kill or injure either man or beast. Just save the horses, that was all.

He fired as soon as he was outside the door. Then Punkin dashed ahead, barking wildly, and Dan fired again. Behind him he could hear Mom calling his name; hear the excited voices of the kids. He started running toward the animals.

"Get out! Get out of here!" he shouted.

Dan could see three men, one on the ground loosening the hobbles of the Osborne horses. He stopped and took aim. He'd shoot just above this fellow's head. Close enough to scare them off, this time. The other two were already circling, rounding up the horses, starting to drive them away.

Dan fired and the shot was answered with a loud curse. It must have been close.

"Get out of here and leave our horses alone!" Dan yelled, but before the words were out of his mouth he heard one of the men speak.

"You all right, Slim?"

The question, voiced in a rough, half-whisper, paralyzed Dan. The gun slid to the ground at his side. Punkin continued barking and in the dull grey light Dan could see the men riding off, driving unmounted horses ahead of them, but he couldn't move. The restaurant in Williston, the gambling room behind the bar and the coarse men at the tables flashed through his mind. He'd thought Slim was tied up with the Interests, but it was worse than that. A horse thief! They hung horse thieves. It was a crime worse than murder in North Dakota. And stealing his own father's horses!

The realization that some of the horses were gone freed

Dan and he started running to the animals. Prince was still there and four others. Well, he'd follow Slim! He'd make him give back those two horses! He had to have them, with haying coming on, and harvest.

Stumbling in the darkness he found the shot gun he had dropped, and a bridle. Mom was calling to him and the dog was racing about wildly, but Dan had no time for either of them.

"Call the dog back," he shouted as he mounted Prince and started after the men who now were well ahead of him.

Dan had ridden almost half an hour before the blood stopped pounding in his temples and he could breathe easily again. He began to think, then. He couldn't see the men ahead but he could hear the pounding hooves. If he guessed right, they were headed for the coulee where Isaiah Parker's sheep had been trapped. It would be a safe place to hide out until dark tomorrow night. They wouldn't be likely to drive stolen horses across the state in daylight.

Dan thought of John Schneider and Mr. Parker. If he could only go to them for help! There were other settlers near the coulee who could be called on too. He'd seen their shacks when he was there before. But Slim was one of those horse thieves! Better let him get away with all the animals in the county than to let anyone know about Slim!

Dan slowed Prince's pace. He'd fall behind until the sound of hooves would be lost in the distance. He was sure of the gang's destination now. They'd be at the coulee before daybreak. He'd try to slip up on their hiding place unobserved. If they were sleeping he might be able to single his own horses out from the others and get them safely away. He remembered the way the coulee lay, and the sharp bend at the entrance to the "U". About a mile to the right there was a gully where he could leave Prince, safely out of sight. When he found it, Dan slipped the hobbles around Prince's fore legs and fastened the buckle securely. Then, gun in hand and crouching low, he inched his way along the top of the hill. If the horses were in the far bend of the "U" and the men on guard at the entrance, he'd have no chance of getting to the animals. He'd have to shoot down at the camp and try to frighten the men out of the hollow. Perhaps they'd be so anxious to save their own skins that they'd leave the animals and he could recover them. But if they had made camp in the seclusion of the "U" and the horses were near the entrance, Dan decided he'd risk everything on trying to recover the animals unobserved. There was no sense in trying to single Slim out and talk to him, as he'd thought at first to do. It made him sick to think of seeing Slim like this.

On the top of the hill ahead Dan could see a dark object like a huge stone. Dropping to his stomach he dragged himself cautiously toward it. The grass rustled beneath his body and every pebble he loosened seemed to grate loudly in the quiet night. After each forward lunge Dan stopped to peer and listen, but the only sound he heard was the rustle of grass moving in the wind and the sniffling of horses in the hollow. From the shelter of the rock ahead he might be able to judge the layout below and know what to do.

Head and shoulders low, gun grasped tightly to his side, Dan made one last forward lunge. The next instant he was jerked to his feet and the gun was out of his hands. A blow sent him spinning, slipping, sliding down on his knees, on the side of the hill. Behind him heavy footsteps and muttered curses.

Dan tried to get to his feet. The best he could hope for

was to run . . . get away in the darkness perhaps. But someone was coming up the hill now, puffing and swearing.

"What the . . ."

An iron hand gripped his arm and once more he was jerked off his feet, sent rolling and sliding to the bottom of the hollow. The two men were over him before he could get up.

"Get in there!"

There was no mistaking the order, for a shove headed Dan into the ravine.

"Get back on watch," one man whispered to the other. "No telling how many he's got following him."

Dan was about to say he was alone but thought better of it. Let them worry about a posse that might be coming! He'd say nothing now until he saw Slim.

He was pushed along to a spot near the entrance which he remembered well. It was here that he had taken leave of Isaiah Parker and ridden off to Williston, light-hearted in the hope of finding Slim. Well, he'd found him. He'd see him again in a few minutes no doubt.

Another ugly shove and Dan was on his knees in the dirt again. "Stay down!" he was told.

"Only one?" Dan heard a new voice ask. It wasn't Slim.

"So far," came the answer. "It'll be daylight in another half hour and we can see what's up."

No one spoke after that, and, crouched against the side of the hill, Dan waited for the sky to lighten. They'd know as soon as morning came that he was alone, for the prairie lay flat for miles in all directions except for this sheltering coulee.

Darkness lightened gradually to a gray mist. A thread of rose on the horizon widened and melted and crept upward. Crouched on the damp ground Dan glanced up and saw how he had been trapped. What had appeared to be a rock on the brow of the hill had been the lookout. Now the fellow was unwinding himself and standing up. Head in his hands, Dan watched as the man stretched, scanned the horizon in all directions, then started down to the camp below. The hulking figure at Dan's side was stirring too. Dan turned and looked into the small, dark eyes of a half-breed Indian. At his side and well out of Dan's reach, lay Pa's gun.

The Indian got up when the lookout reached him.

"See anything?" he asked without a trace of accent.

"No," the man answered, then turning to Dan: "Don't tell me you came alone?"

Nothing was to be gained by lying. Dan nodded and turning from them looked about the coulee. At least ten horses were herded together a few rods beyond them, and lying on a narrow ledge above them, rolled in a blanket, was a third man.

A rough jerk at his shoulder brought Dan's attention back to the men beside him.

"You followed us alone? What for?" the half-breed demanded.

Dan tried to jerk his arm free, but the vise-like grip did not loosen.

"What for?"

Between clenched teeth Dan answered. "You took our horses," he said. "I want to see Slim!"

Dan felt the grip loosen.

"Slim?" both men asked at the same time.

"What do you want to see Slim for?" the half-breed demanded.

"He's my brother," Dan answered defiantly. "He doesn't know it was our horses you took."

He probably didn't care, either, Dan thought after he had said it. But Slim was going to know everything now. About

Pa. About Mom working in the fields like a man. Milking cows. Building barns. If there was any deceny left in Slim, he'd do something now.

The man let Dan's arm go and motioned him to sit down. Reaching for a grain bag he produced a loaf of bread and some slices of cold fried pork. With a huge jack-knife he hacked off the bread and handed slices to his companion and to Dan. They were eating in silence when a footstep startled them. All three looked up at once into the hard, deeply lined face of a huge, lanky man who towered above them.

"Ever see this kid before?" Dan heard the half-breed saying.

Amazed, Dan stared at the stoop-shouldered, bony giant. If he was "Slim" he was not Slim Osborne. Dan scrambled to his feet.

"Are you . . . Slim?" he asked.

For a few seconds the man did not speak. When he did, his questions were punctuated with oaths.

"What's the meanin' of this, Joe?" he demanded of the Indian. "A guest we've got, eh?"

"He said you were his brother," the dark eyed man replied.

"Brother! How many's he got trailin' him?"

"He come alone," the lookout said.

"You sure? Go look again."

Hurriedly the man started up the hill, leaving breakfast behind. A few minutes later he signalled with an outward wave of both hands, but he remained at his post at the top of the hill.

The man called Slim turned on Dan then, and with an unexpected blow sent him reeling into the grass on the floor of the coulee. Before Dan could get to his feet, two bony hands were gripping at his throat.

"You ain't goin' back and put no possee on my trail," the man muttered, his foul breath hot in Dan's face.

Claw-like fingers tightened about Dan's neck. Futilely he struggled to pry back the iron arms; to get to his feet. The air was seeping from his lungs and his chest was like lead. Fighting with all his force he could not free himself from the vicious strangle hold, nor loosen the hands that were choking him to death.

Almost like a voice from another world came the words that saved Dan.

"There'll be no killing, Slim. Let him go."

Dan knew it was Joe who spoke. He gasped as the fingers loosened and the cold air cut his burning lungs. Blindly he steadied himself, then got to his feet.

The men called Slim and Joe were facing each other.

"Who's runnin' these horses?" the thin man demanded.

"You are," came the answer. "But I say there'll be no killing."

"What do you figger to do with him?"

"I'll take care of him tonight when we start," Joe said. "Go eat and leave him with me."

Dan was relieved to know that his fate was in the hands of this half-Indian, half-white man. But a greater relief was the assurance that he had only himself to fear for. That no Osborne was an outlaw.

Long, endless hours of daylight followed. Like the hour hand on a clock the sun moved across the cloudless blue sky. Its warmth was comforting, for Dan was bruised from head to foot. His clothing was torn, his knuckles covered with bloody scabs, and one side of his face was aching from the impact of Slim's last blow.

No one spoke during that anxious day. The men took turns

at climbing to the rim of the coulee where, flat on their stomachs they watched for any sign of discovery. Below, one dozed while the other kept an eye on Dan and the horses. Hungry and thirsty, Dan waited for night, wondering whether Joe would set him free or force him to ride along with the gang.

But the load that had been lifted from Dan's heart was worth the pain and discomfort and anxiety. His brother might be working with the Interests and against the settlers, but he wasn't disgracing the Osborne family.

Now that Dan had time to think of it, he was ashamed that he had ever held the suspicion. If he had only gone to John Schneider and Isaiah Parker and let them know where the gang was hiding out! With a few more to help they could have driven these horse thieves out of the coulee and recovered the horses. How was he ever going to explain what he had done? Never would he tell anyone why he had done it!

Not until the long twilight had faded and the first stars were showing did the three men come together at the entrance to their hideout. Then Slim confronted the half-breed.

"All right, Joe," he sneered. "What're ye figgerin' on doin' with him?"

Joe reached into his pocket and brought out a small box.

"You start the horses out," he said. "Just leave my mare here and I'll catch up with you. The wind's favoring us."

Slim raised his head, as though to catch the direction of the breeze.

"Nobody'll follow us from north or east of the coulee, him included," Joe continued. Then motioning Dan to follow, he started up the hill.

At the top, Joe stopped and lit a match to the grass. Red fingers instantly reached out, curling, spreading, fanned by the night breeze. All along the ridge Joe ran, starting patches of fire, hurrying faster and faster as the flames began to spread. Aghast Dan followed him.

They worked east toward the gully where Dan had left Prince. Would Joe let him keep the horse when they came to him at last? The thought of losing Prince sent a chill through Dan, but he knew he could not fight this man, and Pa's gun was either back in the coulee or hanging from Slim's saddle as he and his lookout rode off to the south and west, headed for the Badlands and the Montana line. The fire would cut off pursuit as Joe had promised. Maybe . . . maybe Joe would let him keep his horse.

Just before they reached the gully the half-breed straightened up and tossing one last match into the dry grass ahead of him, turned back.

"If you're smart you'll get going," he said and with a quick jump started down the side of the hill, back to the place where his own horse had been left.

Dan didn't stop to watch him. Stumbling in the dusk he ran ahead of the fire toward Prince. He'd be there all right. He couldn't have wandered away or the lookout would have seen him.

"Prince!" Dan called under his breath. "Prince!"

The answering whinny was a joy to Dan's ears. In a second the hobbles were off and Dan was riding back, ahead of the flames that now were rising higher in an unbroken wall behind him. He had gone only a short distance when he heard voices, off to the right.

"Here! Come to the east end," someone was shouting.

Dan drew Prince to a halt. Was that Isaiah Parker's voice?

If anyone was responsible for the fire, it was Dan and well he knew it. The least he could do was help fight it. Pulling on the rein sharply he started Prince in the drection of the voices.

"I'm coming," Dan called.

"Come to the east end of the fire," the man called back. "Ma! Where be ye? Go back for more water!"

Hobbling Prince once more, Dan hurried toward the figures now silhouetted against the flaming red wall. It was Isaiah Parker all right and John Schneider and other men he didn't know.

"Grab a grain bag," Mr. Parker ordered, coughing as the smoke choked off his breath. "Ma's gone for more water. Mebee we kin beat it out."

Flailing with all their strength at the creeping belt of fire, the men made slow headway. When Mrs. Parker came back with water for the grain bags they deadened the flames more quickly. But ahead of them the fire was leaping forward and when Dan took time to glance up it seemed it had spread all along the rim of the coulee and far to the westward. The air was filled with the rank smell of burning prairie grass.

"I've gotta save them sheep," Mr. Parker gasped. "You're the Osborne feller, ain't ye? The one that figgered on buyin' 'em?"

"Yes," Dan said. "You still got them?"

Mr. Parker nodded, saving his breath to fight the fire, and did not speak again until they both paused at the water barrel to wet the bags once more.

"I've got 'em yet, but they're sold," Mr. Parker told him then. "Trouble's all they've been. To me and others too. Now I've got to deliver 'em back to the sheep country where I got 'em." Then he hurried back to the smoke and searing heat with Dan beside him.

"We can't stop it this way, Parker," a strange voice finally shouted. "We've got to get back and plow firebreaks around our buildings."

"Not yet! Don't go yet," Mr. Parker begged. "My sheep are spread out all over. I don't know where they all be. Stop this end of the fire first."

"Sheep!" an angry voice protested. "What'd you bring 'em here for anyway? I've got my own place to save."

"I'm takin' 'em out," Mr. Parker almost sobbed. "Help me save 'em so I kin deliver 'em. I've sold 'em."

"Don't go yet," Dan heard Mrs. Parker pleading as he stumbled to the tubs of water in the darkness. "Pa's realized his mistake. He's sold the sheep and he can't lose 'em now. We've got to settle up."

Choking with smoke and miserable with his sense of guilt and responsibility, Dan reached for Mrs. Parker's hand.

"I'll stay with you," he promised.

"Thank God someone will," she whispered. "We've had nothing but trouble. Brought trouble on others too, and it weren't Pa's fault."

For a moment Dan paused.

"Others?" he asked, splashing a few precious drops of water on his burning face. "What others?"

"Pa borrowed on the land and bought sheep instead of farming tools, like the Loan Office thought he was going to do," Mrs. Parker explained as she soaked the grain bag in water for Dan. "They're houndin' him to pay up. Him and his pardner. So now his pardner keeps comin' out and tellin' Pa he's got to settle up 'cause they're takin' it outta him too. Pa never aimed to bring trouble on no one . . . Here!" And she shoved the wet bag into Dan's hand.

Back to the fire then, beating, pounding, holding his head sideways to catch a breath of air. The sweat poured down

Dan's back and legs. Tears filled his eyes. All about him men were coughing, gasping, muttering curses. And to the west the flames were spreading, leaping skyward. The wind was rising too, whipping the fire across the prairie. Oh, Joe was right, for sure! No one would follow the horse thieves from north or east of the coulee.

"It's no use, Parker," one of the men finally gasped. "I'm going back. I can't stay here no longer."

"Just a little longer," Mr. Parker urged. "Ma's gone for more water."

But the men were leaving. Only John Schneider was willing to stay.

"You'll plow a firebreak for me if I stay?" he asked and Mr. Parker quickly agreed.

Dan's back was aching, his face seared and smarting, his eyes swollen almost shut. He straightened and turned his back on the fire, hoping for a breath of clear air. Dimly Mrs. Parker's words came back to him. It was the Interests again. He remembered what Slim had said too. Only how did Slim know about Isaiah Parker?

"Can you pay off what you owe if we save the sheep?" Dan asked Mr. Parker between gasps as they paused once more to soak their bags in the water.

"Enough so they'll let me alone for a spell," was the answer.

"Who?" Dan pressed. "The fellows at the Loan Office?"

It must be someone Slim knew. How else could Slim have heard about Mr. Parker and the sheep, Dan reasoned.

Even in the darkness, with smoke whipping them in the face, Dan again sensed Mr. Parker's reaction. Once more the man was wary and on guard.

"I'll deliver 'em and pay up too," he muttered. "I never beat no one out of nothing. Just help me fight it back another half mile."

"Another half mile," Dan promised but that was as long as he dared to stay. No one was fighting the fire beyond them to the west, where it was racing ahead madly, a wall of gold and red and swirling smoke billowing upward. Dan's own farm lay in its path. He couldn't stay much longer, either.

9. June Primary

PRINCE was frightened. Head tossing wildly, eyes rolling, he was jumping ahead in short, crazy leaps when Dan overtook him almost a mile from the fire.

"There boy! Quiet now!"

But the reassuring tone and firm hand on the bridle had no effect. It was all Dan could do to mount him, and once the hobbles were loosened, Prince immediately streaked across the prairie. The reins flapped uselessly out of reach and Dan clung to the curling mane with both hands, thankful that he was able to stay on the animal's back. Thankful too when the moon rose giving the terrified horse a view of the ground beneath his racing feet. For Prince did not slacken his pace until his sides were flaked with lather, his mouth foaming, and the fire miles behind him.

Dan regained the reins at last and breathed easier. One misstep, one loose stone or unseen badger hole could have thrown him; crippled both horse and rider and left them helpless in the path of the prairie fire. Not until Prince, panting for breath, had slowed to a walk did Dan realize fully the danger in that wild ride.

"Prince, you crazy, fool horse!" he whispered, wiping the cold sweat from his forehead. "Did you think I'd leave you? Abandon you to the fire?" He petted the wet black neck with gentle strokes. "I couldn't abandon Isaiah Parker and his sheep, either."

And he hadn't. The east end of the flames had been beaten back a safe distance before Dan had left the smoke-blackened, exhausted man and his wife. Dan hadn't learned anything more about Isaiah Parker's dealings with the Loan Office in Williston though, nor how Slim had known about the affair.

But Dan had no time to think about that. Peering ahead and trying to judge the distance Prince had covered, Dan suddenly was conscious of a new blaze—a flicker of flame close to the ground straight ahead of him.

Abruptly Dan pulled on the reins, heading Prince to the east so the fires behind and ahead of him were at his back. What was the meaning of this? How could a second fire have started, far to the north of the coulee? It couldn't be much more than five miles from home. He'd have to swing around it. He'd be trapped between two walls of flame if he didn't get ahead of it.

"Come on, boy!" Dan urged slapping the horse's damp flank. "Come on now. You've had time to get your wind."

Glancing back over his shoulder, Dan watched the progress of this second menace. It was spreading to the west, paralleling the blaze behind him. Someone must be deliberately setting it, for the wind would have driven the flames north and east, not west. He'd be able to circle it and get home if he could control Prince. And Prince was docile enough now, too tired to gallop or resist the pull of the reins. Dan talked to him quietly as he rode along, first to the east and then north again, watching all the time for any new sign of danger.

"It's all right, Prince," he kept repeating. "We'll get home in time to plow a firebreak. It's all right."

But was it? Who had started this second blaze and why? Could he cover the miles that separated him from home before the flames were licking at his own house and the barn he hadn't finished? Mom would save the family all right. She'd get Pa and the kids into the wagon and to safety, once she saw the fire. And she'd be up at daylight. What with worrying about him, gone two nights now, likely she hadn't slept at all, nor Pa either. They'd see the crackling flames and hear the roar of it on the hot wind in time to save themselves. If only he could get home in time to plow a firebreak and save the house and barn!

Once more Dan slapped at Prince's flanks. He had to get home! Once more the long black legs reached out over the miles. Hazy daybreak reddened the eastern sky, smoke and crawling destruction colored the morning mist to the right, as Dan turned west at last, safely ahead of the second fire, safe on his way home.

It wasn't long before Dan recognized the pigmy size of the second blaze. No towering, flickering wall of red, no wildly billowing smoke here. At the end nearest him there were only smouldering embers and low-hanging clouds of smoke. Cautiously he headed Prince nearer and soon he understood. Ten wide, black furrows of freshly plowed earth stretched to the west alongside the burning grass. Someone had seen the danger hours ago. More than one man had been plowing half the night, setting small grass fires beyond the furrows to widen the firebreak.

Dan followed the black road west. This was the work of the Nelsons and Jim Jackson and maybe Ernst and Peter. He came upon them at last, a black-faced, sweating army bending low over plows, pushing the firebreak north now. It would protect all of the claims in the neighborhood and a wide stretch of public domain too, where Dan and the others had planned to cut hay next month.

"Chris! Nels!" Dan shouted as he hurried up to them.

The Nelson boys called to him at once, and Jim Jackson and Mr. Nelson turned to wave.

"Hello there, you daredevil!" Jim called to him, but no one stopped plowing even for a minute. Behind them the Germans were setting the back fires, keeping each patch of flame under control, watching lest the wind fan sparks across the band of black earth. They shouted and waved, too, but no one stopped. And far ahead of all of them a slim figure, doubled over plow handles, blazed the trail that would save the homes of them all. Dan strained his eyes in the dim morning light. Who was that? Certainly the horses were the Osborne's own bays. He'd followed those broad, swaying rumps for too many hours not to know them. But who . . . ?

Dan pulled along side Chris, the last in the staggered line of plowmen.

"What happened to you?" Chris demanded excitedly. "Where've you been?"

"There were horse thieves. I followed them." Dan explained.

"That I know," Chris answered. "But where have you been?"

"Hiding out in a coulee south of here," Dan explained.

"They caught me and held me all day yesterday. Then they set the fire last night so no one could follow them."

Nels, head cocked to one side to hear the conversation, was nodding.

"That's what Tom figured," he called back. "We hunted for you all day yesterday."

"Tom?" Dan asked. "Where's he now?" But as he asked the question his eyes went ahead to the lead team.

"Yeah, that's him," Chris announced. "If it hadn't been for him we'd never of got started plowing in time. He'd stayed at our house for supper after we got home from hunting for you, and the minute we saw that fire he knew what was up."

Dan pushed the hair out of his eyes. Tom had been hunting for him. Tom had seen the fire and had known what to do.

"You won't believe it," Chris went on pushing his plow forward as he talked. "You should have heard him telling Paw what to do and how the neighbors should get organized. When he went for Jim Jackson he stopped at your place and got your plow and horses. You've got four horses left, you know."

Dan knew. Four horses to do the work of six, with haying and harvest coming on. He rode in silence beside the staggered line of plowmen, each one trailing slightly behind the one ahead, each one cutting two furrows at once. Tom had planned all this and was leading the line.

"Where's his old man?" Dan finally asked.

"Don't bring that up," Chris warned. "He must-a brought a bottle or two home from Minot. No one's seen him and I guess this once Tom was glad."

That explained how Tom had been free to search for Dan and to round up the neighbors.

"Maybe I ought to ride up and offer to relieve him," Dan suggested.

"Don't do that," Chris advised. "He don't want to be relieved. What you'd better do is get home before your Maw loses her mind."

Chris was right, Dan knew. Besides, he was suddenly very tired. It was the thought of Mom and home that did it. For two days and two nights he'd scarcely slept at all, and he wished he could drop to the ground, safe within the firebreak and go to sleep. So he rode ahead and stopped only for a few seconds when he came to Tom.

"You've sure got it licked," Dan called.

Tom scarcely looked up. "We've got a long ways to go yet," he announced. "Past our place yet."

Tom wasn't grinning. His thin face was determined looking, his lips pulled tight across his teeth. He was pushing at the plow handles as though the lives of all of them depended on him and the furrows he was knifing northward. Well, he was doing a good job and Dan had no wish to take any of the credit from him. He headed Prince toward home and let the reins fall limp and his body sag.

The last miles were endless. Half-green, half-gray the prairie grass moved in a sleepy haze ahead of him. Like a blanket the rising sun warmed his head and shoulders. Larks, prairie hens, and gophers all were moving along with him, away from the smoke and fire, but Dan was scarcely conscious of them. When he lifted his eyes it was to measure the narrowing distance between himself and home, and when Prince walked the last long rods toward the house, when Punkin's barks and Eddie's shrieks brought Mom and Grace running, Dan could only slide off the horse and stumble toward them.

He slept the clock around. Singing hammers wakened him at last and he sat up with a jerk, feeling strange at finding himself in Pa's bed, then conscious of the dirt and smoke and sweat that covered him uncomfortably. He shook his head and listened. All that noise! Who was helping Mom with the barn? Then kitchen noises told him Mom was in the house and the smell of coffee got him to his feet eagerly. What was going on?

It was a dirty and dishevelled Dan who stood in the kitchen doorway a moment later, staring at Mom up to her elbows in bread dough, and Petra peeling baskets of potatoes.

"Are you a sight!" Petra grinned. Her hair was pulled back out of the way, and she looked for all the world like Chris. "They told me, but I couldn't imagine it."

Dan rubbed uncomfortably at his face, and looked at the snags and rips in his trousers, at his smoke-blackened arms and hands, covered with bloody scabs. Then he glanced inquiringly toward the yard and the noises and voices.

"It's a barn raising," Mom explained. "But you've got to have a bath before anyone sees you. I've got water hotting. Give me a hand."

As they carried the washtub back into the bedroom Mom glanced at him cautiously.

"Did they hurt you much?" she whispered.

"Not much," Dan assured her. "I got off pretty easy."

She stood by the tub a moment, the towels over her shoulders, and the cake of soap in her hand trembled. "Tell me the truth, Dan," she whispered. "I heard. When they drove the horses off, I heard."

She was looking at him appealingly and her face was drawn and gray looking. Dan knew immediately what she meant.

"It wasn't him, Mom," he assured her. "I thought it was and that's why I followed. But it wasn't him."

Mom was swallowing hard and the tears were running down her face. She wiped her eyes with the towels she had brought for Dan.

"It was worth getting beat up for, just to know it wasn't our Slim," he told her. "Did Pa hear? Does he . . ."

"I'll tell him," Ma said. "I'll let him know right away."

Dan wondered, as he scrubbed himself clean and dressed in the fresh clothes Mom had laid out for him, whether the Germans were out at the barn, and Ike and Tom and Jim Jackson. He listened to the voices and heard all except Tom's. When he finally went into the yard a chorus of cheers went up and Dan stared in amazement at the men.

"Silver trophies is what we should have," Mr. Nelson said with his slow smile. "For you and Tom both."

Dan looked around the yard. "Where is Tom?" he asked.

"Getting food for us," Chris said. "We never appreciated Tom and that's for sure."

Ike Sheets, sober now, smiled patronizingly. Hammer in hand, he was making a show of working.

"Food?" Dan asked.

"Oh, your folks had plenty for everyone except meat, so Tom's over there getting pheasants," Chris explained. Nels, working beside his younger brother, only nodded.

Dan looked toward the edge of the wheat field, lush and green in the sun, untouched by the fire. He could see Tom crouching at the edge of the grain and he waited for the sound of his gun. But no shot was fired and as Dan watched he saw Tom rise cautiously to his knees, left hand even with his eyes, right hand back beyond his shoulder.

"I never seen a boy with his deadly aim," old man Sheets

was saying. "He kin bring 'em down every time. One right after the other. There'll be a fat bird for every man here in an hour's time."

Slowly Dan realized how Tom was doing it. Sharp stones in a sling shot. No frightening shots to alarm the other birds. And as he watched, the blood began to pound in his temples and he felt his cheeks grow hot. Prince . . . a stone in a sling shot could have hurtled through the air silently, from Ike Sheets' wagon to the grazing horses, the night when Prince had broken away!

Dan turned from the men to his father's wheel chair. He wished he hadn't seen it. Wished he didn't know. He'd talk to Pa for a minute and collect himself, before he found a hammer and joined the others. Tom had won their admiration for the first time. He couldn't show how he felt, or let anyone know of the distrust that Tom's skill had awakened. Not now.

Dan realized, as he walked to the wheel chair, that his father had been watching him. The good right hand was reaching out to him and Pa's grip was firm and comforting.

"Maybe . . . you're wrong," Pa said quietly. "About . . . Tom, too."

Dan breathed deeply. Pa was telling him more than the few words said. Telling him that he knew why Dan had followed the horse thieves, knew that Slim wasn't one of them. It was a new bond between them, those few words.

But it didn't drive the rankling distrust from Dan's heart and he had little to say as he joined the men at the barn. Once, as he lifted a side board into place he looked up in time to see Nels observing him carefully. Dan didn't avoid his eyes and in that second he knew that Nels, the quiet one, shared his doubt. It didn't make Dan any happier but it was a relief to know that he was not the only one who felt there still was an answer to be given, perhaps a score to be settled.

All that day Old Man Sheets was busier being friendly than with building the barns. Downright fatherly he was as he slapped Jim Jackson on the shoulder and talked to Peter and Ernst, and praised Dan whenever he had the opportunity.

"Brave boy, Dan," he kept saying. "Not many'd dare follow horse thieves," and he'd shake his head as though it was a deed quite beyond his comprehension. Even Tom seemed embarrassed and Dan was outright disgusted. It was plain enough that Ike didn't want to lose his hold on the men he was counting on, with the primary coming up. When Mom and Petra spread the table in the shade of the house, loading it with mashed potatoes, roasted game birds, hot bread and green vegetables from Pa's garden, Ike beamed and rubbed his hands together and praised Mom too.

"Not another cook in the whole state of North Dakota like your Missus, Osborne," he said to Pa. "She allus does it now, doesn't she?"

"You may be disappointed when it comes to dessert," Mom said modestly. "You men folks surprised me entirely this time and I couldn't turn out bread and pies both. So all you'll get is molasses cookies and stewed fruit."

But Mom's molasses cookies! She made them with sour cream and they were soft and sweet and would melt in your mouth. She must have baked them yesterday, Dan figured, but they'd be just as good as the minute they came out of the oven. How the men pounced on them, cleaning up plate after plateful. When she set the table for supper, she had pies for them too. There were baked beans, steaming hot and juicy, with bits of salt pork on top; potato salad and devilled eggs, and the juicy pies made of dried apples and dried peaches.

"Would you folks like a barn dance tonight?" Mom asked as she passed the food. "Petra tells me Nels played the accordion and Dan's real good with the guitar."

The shout that went up was answer enough.

"Nels, I didn't know you had an accordion," Dan gasped in surprise. Then turning to Ernst, "Ride home and get your fiddle, quick. Gee, how we could use some more girls. Petra, you should have been twins!"

Petra beamed at him. "Help carry in the dishes," she ordered.

Once inside the kitchen she turned to Dan, suddenly serious.

"Dan . . ."

"What, Petra?"

"Would you . . . Do you suppose . . ."

Dan set the dirty dishes on the kitchen table.

"I never knew you to be bashful before," he said. "What's the matter?"

"I was just thinking about Mama," Petra said, and her voice was almost a whisper. "She loves the music and dancing. She dances all the Norwegian dances just beautiful! I couldn't stay here and leave her home . . . to hear the music but not to dance."

"Why Petra, of course not," Dan said. "Didn't Mom tell you to get her? Mom wouldn't leave her out. You know Mom isn't like that!"

"She told me but . . . but would you. . . . Would Peter. . . ."

Dan was sure what Petra meant. Her mother couldn't speak a word of English. Would the men ask her to dance?

"Look, Petra, you go get your mother," Dan said. "Make her come. Tell her I want the first dance."

"You've got to play," Petra reminded him. Then before he knew what was happening she threw her arms around his waist, hugged him until he lost his breath, and then ran bareheaded from the house.

Mrs. Nelson couldn't speak English but she could dance, and Dan could scarcely take his eyes off her. As the music started she locked her two hands behind Mr. Nelson's neck and smiled happily as she looked up at him. Taking a firm grip at her neat waist he whirled her off her feet, around and around the floor. Blonde braids soon were flying behind her, blue eyes flashing happiness, as her full skirt ballooned around the room. Close behind were Chris and Petra seriously tripping the same old Norwegian dance and patterning as best they could their dancing parents.

It was the first time Dan and Nels and Ernst ever had played together, but there were enough tunes that they all knew to keep the dancing going. Before the night was out, Pa was calling square dances, Peter Myers was squiring Mom around the barn, and Tom was curtseying to Grace. Everyone was dancing.

When midnight came, Mom and Mrs. Nelson and Mrs. Jackson had more food for the men. Big plates of sandwiches, three kinds of cake, and coffee.

Dan glanced at his mother and shook his head. How had she managed to plan it all? Whenever had she baked those cakes? How had she done it? Ike Sheets could out-talk Pa all right, but he couldn't out-do Mom.

She was ready for him, two weeks later too, when the men in the county began to gather at the Osborne barn to vote in the primary election. It was Mr. Nelson who had suggested holding the primary at the Osborne place so Pa wouldn't have to struggle to get in and out of the wagon in order to go somewhere else to cast his vote. Mr. Nelson had arranged it weeks before, when the county commissioners got out the election notices and Ike had been agreeable to it then. But that was before Petra had spread the word about Pa teaching school, and before the horse thieves had come to the neighborhood.

"Now that some of the neighbors feel that maybe they owe us something Ike wishes he hadn't gone along with Mr. Nelson," Mom had told Dan as she scrubbed Grace's ears and combed her hair, braiding the pigtails neatly. "He's been campaigning against Pa, but he's not so sure of his votes as he was."

"You sure?" Dan asked as he got fresh water from the teakettle on the back of the kitchen range.

"I hear things," Mom said knowingly. "Jim Jackson won't vote for Pa, but a lot of others favor him for school commissioner now. Most folks, I think."

"What makes you say Jim won't vote for Pa?" Dan said. "He was friendly enough at the barn raising. I talked to him then."

"Mrs. Jackson wasn't. She hardly had a word to say."

"Well, Mrs. Nelson didn't say anything at all," Dan said. "It was the first time she's ever been here for that matter."

"Now Dan, that's no comparison and you know it," Mom said. "Mrs. Nelson sends Petra to help me with everything. Pa'll be teaching school next week, thanks to her. Now Grace, run along and put on your clean dress."

Mom was right and Dan couldn't dispute it. Petra had spent two days riding about the county telling people of the plan to start school this first summer.

"Furthermore," Mom said, "I'm going to see if we can't teach Mrs. Nelson enough English so she won't think she has to stay home by herself. Just as soon as the work slackens. Pa and I'll both be teaching school," she said and laughed to herself at the thought of it.

Bent low over the wash bench Dan splashed away vigorously and let her talk.

"And another thing," Mom went on as she laid out freshly ironed shirts for Pa and Dan and Eddie. "Just as soon as the election's over we've got to find out where the circuit rider goes when he comes out this way. They have church services other places. We need the word of God in this neighborhood bad as anywhere else in North Dakota. Now hurry up and get dressed, and make sure Eddie's washed his neck and ears."

Voting didn't start until late in the afternoon. Most of the near-by neighbors waited until they saw the rigs coming from the far end of the county, then they began coming all at once, with Ike Sheets and Jim Jackson first to arrive. The county commissioners, Ike announced, were in charge of the election and he had the ballots.

Mom had the yard all raked neat, and boards set up to make a table in the shade along side the barn. Nobody knew what she had in her mind until most of the people were there, standing around outside, no one wanting to be the first to go inside and cast his vote. Then from the kitchen Grace appeared, her little blue and white gingham dress all starched and standing out neat. She was carrying a big basket and behind her came Eddie, one shoulder bent over under the weight of the water pail. Dan knew in a minute what was up. Mom had baked a batch of her golden molasses cookies and the water pail was filled with cold switchel. Would that taste good! Ginger and sugar and lemon juice in the cold spring water. Now wasn't that just like Mom!

The kids knew what they were supposed to do. Right to the table they went and Grace spread out the cookies, trying hard not to giggle. She had turned to help Eddie lift the pail to the table when Ike Sheets spoke up.

"Now what's this?" he demanded walking straight up to Pa. "What's this trick you folks is up to?"

The men who had been smiling as they watched the children, were suddenly sober. Ike Sheets' face was ugly. Plainly he was mad.

"Trick?" Pa repeated. "No trick . . . Mrs. Osborne . . . just baked . . ."

But he had no chance to finish the sentence.

"I kin see what she's done," Ike fairly shouted and he seemed to tower over Pa in his wheel chair. "Set out to influence the voters! Feedin' 'em! Paradin' her two kids in front of 'em when their Paw's runnin' for school commissioner! It's electioneerin', that's what it is."

Dan didn't see how Pa remained so calm. Everyone else was tense and worried looking, especially Jim Jackson. Jim was rubbing his hands against his pants and swallowing again and again, and staring at the ground. He was on Ike Sheets' side plain enough, but he didn't look like it was where he wanted to be.

"Now look here, Osborne," Ike continued, "You get them kids outa here with whatever they've got. It's agin the law to be electioneerin' at the polls. I went along with allowin' you to have the votin' at your place on account of you being all crippled up, but I didn't count on no such trick as this."

Dan felt his cheeks burning. Pa crippled up! Well, it was

true enough, but no one had ever said it before, not to Pa's face. And Pa'd been getting better right along.

Dan glanced around at the voters. He didn't know all of them but it seemed to him they were all staring right at him. He went over and stood beside Pa, who had turned away from Ike and was motioning to Grace and Eddie. The kids were standing by the table, frightened now. Eddie's eyes were wide and dark with alarm and Grace's lips were trembling.

"Go back . . . to the house," Pa said to them.

"And take your stuff with you!" Ike fairly yelled at them. "Take it and get out!"

It was Grace who started to run. She paid no attention to Ike Sheets but rushed straight to Pa and clung to his knees crying. Eddie remained beside the pail of switchel at the table.

"Stop your blubberin'!" Ike scolded angrily. "This is no place for kids. The county commissioners is runnin' this election, not you nor your Maw. Now get outa here, both of you."

No one raised a voice against Ike Sheets. Dan looked about for Mr. Nelson. He was a county commissioner too. He ought to do something. But he hadn't come yet and Jim Jackson wasn't saying a word. Pa was stroking Grace's head, trying to quiet her, and the only sound in the barnyard was the cackling and clucking of the hens.

"Pa, shall I take the kids to the house?" Dan asked.

But before Pa could answer Ike had Grace by the shoulder, trying to shove her away from Pa. She jerked and cried out and fought to keep her hold on Pa's knees. Ike gave another tug at her shoulder, whirling her around, but she flung herself back at her father. Then Ike grabbed at the wheel chair and in another second it careened to one side and dipped and swayed and went over in a crash of splintering wood and metal grating against pebbles in the yard.

For one horrified instant Dan stared at Pa, sprawled helplessly in the grass, Grace on her knees beside him, shrieking hysterically. Then he and Ernst Schneider were bending over Pa, getting him up between them. Peter had the wheel chair righted and pushed it up against Pa's trembling legs. The back was wrenched loose but the wheels were still intact.

Pa's face was white. Beads of perspiration trickled down his forehead as he sat down slowly and took the handkerchief that Ernst had pulled from his own pocket and handed to him. He didn't say anything. Nobody spoke.

The blood was pounding in Dan's head, throbbing behind his eyes. Turning from Pa he swung at Ike Sheets with all the force in his body, and struck the man square on the chin. In an instant Ike was at him, arms flailing, fists landing blows on Dan's head and shoulders. But Dan felt only rage and hatred as he fought back. Snarling and cursing Ike knocked him off his feet more than once but each time Dan was up before Ike could pounce upon him . . . up and beating at his bull-like antagonist . . . Maybe he can lick me . . . Maybe he can kill me . . . but not until I've given him what he's got coming . . .

The heavy hulk closed in and blows pelted Dan's back and shoulders. But Ike was breathing hard and as Dan landed an upper cut, Ike reeled back. Then Dan heard Mr. Nelson's voice behind him.

"There can't be fighting at the polls."

Mr. Nelson and Jim Jackson separated them.

Dan shook himself free of the hands that held him and turned to Pa. Peter was holding the wheel chair together, and had pushed Pa part way back to the house. Eddie and

Grace were with him and Mom was running across the yard.

"Pa!" she kept saying over and over again. "Pa, are you all right?"

Mom was frightened to death! Her face was fairly gray and she seemed not to see anyone but Pa.

Dan took the wheel chair from Peter and carefully wheeled Pa back to the house. Safe inside the kitchen he put his arms under Pa's shoulders and helped him to his bed, while Mom hurried to the drawer where she kept the medicines.

"The doctor said if anything ever upset you, to give you this, Pa," she said handing him a pill and a glass of water.

"I'm not . . . upset," Pa said. "Just . . . shaken up a mite." But he took the pill Mom offered and lay back on the bed and closed his eyes.

Dan and Mom went to the kitchen then and sat down helplessly at the table. Grace had stopped her crying and was finding comfort in Punkin's nuzzling head. Eddie stood in the kitchen doorway staring back at the men in the barnyard, his fists clenched and his face white and sober. Dan could see them, too, as they went into the barn, one at a time. As each man came out he joined those who had voted ahead of him, and they formed a silent circle in the shade of the building. No one was touching the cookies and the switchel on the table, though.

Dan glanced at Mom. She was holding her head in her tanned and knotted hands. The finger nails were broken and there were scars where jags and bruises had left their mark. As he watched, tears trickled between her fingers and her shoulders shook a little, but she held back the sobs.

Dan stared at the blue checkered table cloth. He wished he could cry, too. Mom had meant well. She'd fought Ike Sheets with the best weapon she had, but it had been a near disaster to do it. If Pa wasn't any the worse, though, everything would be all right. What did the election matter? Pa would probably lose, now. The last thing the voters had seen was his impotent body stretched in the grass and gravel in his own barnyard. But even if he was defeated the Osborne's hadn't lost anything, Dan reasoned. The wheel chair could be mended. And Ike Sheets had shown himself up for what he was, in front of everybody in the county.

The barnyard and the election grew remote and unimportant as Dan sat beside his mother in the kitchen. All that mattered was Pa. Outside the meadow larks still were singing. Insects chirped and the perfume of a thousand wild rose clusters filled the June air. Beyond the barn a light green sea rolled rhythmically as the wind swayed the growing wheat.

Time became unimportant, too, and the slow chimes of the grandfather's clock stirred no action in the quiet room. When the voting was over and the men had gone there'd be time enough to do the chores.

10. *Squatter Smith*

NOT once as the afternoon shadows stretched out from the house did Mom look into the barnyard. She dried her tears at last and went to the stove to lay a fire for supper and put the teakettle on. From the cooler she brought out a pan of potatoes that had been boiled in their skins and began to peel them.

Chin in hand, long legs stretched out under the table, Dan watched the last of the men go into the barn and come out again. Then Ike and Jim and Mr. Nelson went in, taking two others with them and Dan judged that the ballots were being counted. It wouldn't take long. Half an hour; an hour at most.

"Want me to go to the garden for anything, Mom?" Dan asked.

"No need," she answered without looking from her work.

Dan got up and walked to the other side of the room where

the windows faced the east and the empty prairie. Those men from off across the county . . . what had they thought? How had they voted? Most of them had never been at the Osborne farm before but some had been at the Nelsons the night the county commissioners were elected. Pa hadn't shown up to very good advantage that night either. Maybe some had sensed then that he was trying to oppose the scheme Ike had worked out to get himself in control of the county business; that Jim Jackson would do just what Ike told him to do, leaving Mr. Nelson in the minority. Maybe some had sensed that Pa had brains. But how many would vote for him now?

It began to matter, as Dan thought about it soberly. It was going to be humiliating to Pa if they all turned against him. How many could he count on? Ernst . . . Peter . . . Mr. Nelson . . . Anyone else?

Restlessly Dan walked about the big room, kitchen in one end and living room in the other, separated only by the stairway leading to the bedrooms above. He ran his fingers across the keys of Mom's organ, sat in the big red plush chairs and on the sofa, then went back to the kitchen for a drink from the water pail and another look into the yard.

The commissioners came out of the barn at last followed by the men who had helped them. They went to the group of voters who were squatted on the grass, leaning against wagon wheels or stretched out in the slivers of shade cast by the sideboards. Everyone got up. Dan couldn't see who was talking.

"Whatever happened, it's over now," he said to his mother but she didn't answer.

It was Mr. Nelson who finally separated himself from the crowd and started toward the house.

"Mr. Nelson's coming, Mom," Dan reported.

"It would have to be him," Mom answered. "Whatever he has to tell us, Dan, there's to be no bitterness shown."

Dan waited in the doorway, trying to glimpse Mr. Nelson's expression, watching the crowd in the yard.

"No one's leaving," he said in a low voice. "No one, that is but Ike and Jim. They're starting off across the field together."

That could mean anything, and the wide brim of Mr. Nelson's hat cast a shadow over his face, hiding his eyes and mouth. Dan's hand shook as he held the screen door open and watched Mr. Nelson remove his hat before he stepped inside. His heart was pounding and his lips dry as the county commissioner looked about the room as though expecting to see Pa, and then turned to Mom.

"Mrs. Osborne, I'm a proud man to be bringing the election news to you," he said. "Where's the Mister?"

Mom went to him eagerly.

"I've got him lying down." It was almost a whisper. Her lips were parted as though she would say more but she waited for him to talk.

"Then I'll leave it to you to tell him when he gets up," Mr. Nelson said. "There was only three votes against him. One of the men from off East got here late or there'd only been two."

Dan did not try to check his sigh of relief and Mr. Nelson smiled as he turned back to the door.

"I told the fellows I'd see if he felt like coming out," he said, "but they'll understand. There'll only be two votes against him in November. Nomination on the Republican ticket is good as being elected in this state."

It was all Mom and Dan could do to voice their thanks.

Out in the yard the men were devouring the cookies and drinking the switchel.

"I can't see why Jim thinks he's got to stand with Ike Sheets," Dan managed to say at last. "I don't believe Ike can help him with the Interests any more than you or Pa, if worst comes to worst."

The shaggy white eyebrows raised a little.

"He's young," Mr. Nelson said. "He never had experience with money or business before. Or elections either. He believes everything Ike's told him. If I'd got here a little earlier . . ." Then he shook his head as though admitting to himself that nothing could have swayed Jim, nor curbed Ike's anger either, once he realized that Mom and circumstances were going to defeat him.

After that Mom could talk about nothing except finding the circuit rider.

"We owe it to the Lord," she insisted.

June was the month for starting the school, for getting haying and harvest tools, for dickering with Ernst and Peter for help at harvest time. And it was the time for Dan to set out on his errand, so once more he borrowed a saddle and blankets from the Nelsons and with a supply of food packed in an old flour sack, he set off across the prairie.

New country lay ahead. Country Dan had not explored. Go far enough and there were lakes he'd heard. But as he rode along he began to doubt it. Just prairie land. Endless, flat land dotted with myriad wild rose clusters now, and here and there a trifling hill rising above a weed-choked gully. He could see the horizon in all directions.

It was mid afternoon when Dan first saw a spire of smoke at the top of a hill ahead of him. There wasn't a sign of a house, but close by a horse was grazing. It had been a long time

since Dan had seen any sign of human habitation and un-
hesitatingly he started toward the spot. Someone must be
camping in a hollow below the hill. He'd ride up and see what
sort of camp it was and what the fellow looked like. But the
nearer he came the more puzzled he was for the smoke was
rising straight out of the earth with no sign of a fire at all.
Dan was fairly over it before he spied the inch or two of
stovepipe sticking above the ground.

Swinging Prince around, Dan rode slowly along the edge
of the hill until he could look down into the gully. There
he saw a cave-like sod shanty built into the hillside and in front
of it a be-whiskered man was crouching low. As Dan watched
he rose slowly, left hand up even with his eyes, right hand
back of his shoulder as, sling shot in hand, he took aim. Black
and white and rufous plumage rose and fell in the grass ahead
of him. Instinctively Dan winced as he recalled the last time
he had seen that deadly gesture. He drew Prince to a halt and
watched. Once more the lethal aim and another bird was
bagged.

Dan was not sure whether the man had seen him as he rose
from his half-crouching position and started across the swale
without a glance in Dan's direction. For a moment he hesitated. The man might take offense if he discovered Dan
when he returned with the birds. He might think Dan had
been spying upon him. Besides, there was a well below and
a wooden water tub, and for hours Prince had been travelling
in the hot sun without a drink.

"Hello!" Dan called. "Can I water my horse here?"

The man turned slowly and shading his eyes with his hand,
looked up at Dan. He was thin and stoop-shouldered and it
was hard to tell where black hair left off and black beard

began. His clothes hung on him, sizes too large for the frame they covered.

"Help yourself," came the answer.

Dan started Prince down into the hollow. It wasn't a very cordial welcome but he hadn't been ordered off the place.

And what a place it was! Stretching in front of the shanty door was a green lawn, marked off with field stones. Stone-lined paths led to the well and to a vegetable garden beyond it. It must have taken weeks to gather the rocks and mark off the lawn and garden. The man must have been watering it every night all summer or the long hours of sunshine would have seared and dulled the grass. It was like a city lawn, that button of green, on the endless sage-grey prairie. The hillside near the shanty was pink with wild roses. Nowhere had Dan seen so many bushes clustered in one place. Some were more than three feet high and he wondered if nature alone had planted them there. Their fragrance filled the air as he rode into the hollow.

But most surprising of all were the cats that played or slept in the sun in front of the shanty. There were a dozen at least; gray pussy cats and black ones and yellow tigers and tiny kittens spotted with white, their tails pointed skyward as they chased each other across the lawn. Dan was still watching them when the man came back, a rabbit and two prairie chickens in his hands. He walked with a slight limp and when Dan smiled, looking from him to his pets, his only response was to gesture toward one of two big stones in his tidy front yard. It was hard to guess his age. He might be 35 or 50.

Dan sat down and the man busied himself skinning the rabbit. His cats ran to him setting up a crescendo of hungry demands.

—134—

"You go hunt your own," he scolded gently. "This one's for Meliss and Mandy."

"Meliss and Mandy," Dan repeated. "Have you a family?" The man shook his head.

"Meliss and Mandy've just had kittens. That's why I favor them. I should have milk for them."

He had a smooth, flowing voice that reminded Dan of a teacher he'd had back in Cincinnati. He looked like a person who'd be satisfied with his cats and his horse, and he certainly didn't seem at all interested in Dan.

"You've fixed this place up nice," Dan said after a few minutes. The man was cutting the white rabbit meat into pieces and tossing them to the cats. He didn't even look up.

"I've got my last 10 acres plowed and in," he said. "Maybe you noticed."

Dan hadn't really noticed the field until then. Only a haphazard attempt had been made at cultivating the land and the thin rows of grain which Dan could identify as oats, were little higher than the prairie grass that surrounded them. There wasn't a sign of a farm tool in the yard but at the edge of the field an old, single-blade plow lay on its side, dropped at the spot where the last furrow ended. The law had been complied with though when the ground was broken and a crop put in, whether there was a harvest or not.

Dan looked back at the man and his cats. He wished he could get the fellow to talking. This was a strange place for sure. How was he figuring on harvesting his crop if he had any crop at all?

"How far is it to the nearest neighbor?" Dan finally asked.

"Six, seven miles I guess. Here, Meliss. You should have milk, I know."

In the bag of food Mom had given Dan, there was a quart

jar of milk. Well, he'd give it to the cats and then if the man wouldn't talk there'd be nothing to do but ride on. So Dan walked back to the well where he had left Prince and got it.

"Here," he said holding out the jar. "I'll just take a drink of water and move on."

The blue-gray eyes that looked at Dan were questioning. Carefully the man lay the rabbit back on the piece of skin and wiped his stained hands on the pheasant feathers at his feet. Dan expected him to reach for the jar of milk but he hesitated.

"Going far?" he finally asked.

"Not much farther," Dan replied. "There's a community east of here, I'm told. A school . . . a store, I guess." Dan didn't really know how large the place was. "How far is it, do you know?"

The man looked from Dan to Prince, taking stock of the horse.

"You can make it by sundown," he said, then glancing at the milk, "Sure you don't need it?"

"I'm sure," Dan said and put the jar on the stone that had served as a chair. "I may pick up the fruit jar on my way back. They aren't easy to come by, out here."

"Wait. I'll get a sauce pan."

He limped across the lawn and into the dimness of his shanty. In a few seconds he was back with a tin basin, shining clean in the sun. Deliberately he poured the milk out and handed the fruit jar back to Dan.

"Meliss and Mandy'll welcome the milk," was all he said.

Dan walked back to the well, washed out his fruit jar and filled it with water. Clearly enough he might as well be on his way. The man had not welcomed his visit and wasn't going to be friendly so he mounted Prince and rode out of the gully with a wave of farewell that was returned with the barest gesture.

But Dan hadn't seen nor heard the last of the strange settler in the hollow. He wondered about the man as he rode the last miles toward the settlement and almost the first words he heard when he arrived there concerned him.

In the dusk the school house, with its bell turret, stood out plainly among the little cluster of buildings. There was a pump and watering trough in the yard, so Dan stopped there. The brash grating of the pump handle brought half a dozen barefooted children running from lighted doorways. They stopped, uncomfortably, when they found a stranger at the well.

"You here for the meeting?" the largest boy finally asked.

Dan hadn't heard anything about a meeting, but he hesitated to admit it before these knowing youngsters.

"You're expecting people, aren't you?" he asked.

"Sure!" It was a chorus.

"Mike thought you wuz Squatter Smith," one boy piped up, then giggled and dodged as the older boy turned on him and started to chase him from the school yard.

"Squatter Smith," Dan repeated. "Hey, wait a minute. Is he the fellow with the black beard?"

"That's him," the youngsters announced. Then "He's addle brained." "He's hiding out." "He'll be at the meeting, though."

"He'll be at the meeting?" Dan repeated, addressing the question to Mike.

"He likes to hear the men from the college talk," Mike explained. "John Worst's here this time."

It was a few seconds before the significance of the name came to Dan. Then he remembered. John Worst was president of the State Agriculture College at Fargo. Mom was forever quoting him. Was John Worst really coming to the meeting?

Mike answered the question before Dan asked it.

"He's staying at our house tonight," Mike said proudly. "Folks from the college always stay at our house. Say, what's your name?"

"Dan Osborne. What's yours?"

"Mike Welch. That's my Pa's name, too."

Then the other children told their names and little by little Dan learned more about the meeting. The farmers in the neighborhood had heard that the College might conduct meetings or Institutes for people who couldn't go to Fargo to attend classes, and they had asked John Worst to come and explain it to them.

"A lot of folks come tonight," Mike explained. "They're all camped down by the straw stacks. You can camp there, too."

In the dusk Dan could see the outline of the stacks. He took Prince's reins and led him from the school yard.

There were other men camped there as the children had said and already they had rolled themselves in their blankets for the night. Quietly Dan lay down close to the sheltering mound of straw and gazed up into the star-swept sky. Squatter Smith . . . criminal? Addle-brained? There was something mysterious about him. And all those cats.

The smell of coffee boiling and bacon frying wakened Dan in the morning. In a few minutes the men were visiting over their camp-fire breakfasts. Few had come from as great a distance as Dan and they exchanged news of crops and the weather and threshing problems eagerly. All of them looked to the Agriculture College with the same unquestioning faith as Mom herself. What John Worst said was almost holy writ.

"He's one man who's for the farmers," Dan heard over and over again.

"Has he been a farmer himself?" Dan asked.

"He's been everything. Took up a homestead in Emmons County in 1883," one man told Dan.

"He was county superintendent of schools two terms and then they sent him to the State Senate," another volunteered. "He served in the Senate until 1895 and then he was elected Lieutenant Governor. He knows what a farmer's up against, first hand. All about politics, too."

"How long has he been president of the Agriculture College?" Dan asked.

"He got that appointment the winter he was made Lieutenant Governor," was the answer. "He's been working for the farmers all those years, in one way or another."

By that time the men were putting out their fires and moving to the school yard. Near-by neighbors were gathering and all the children in the community were racing about, shouting and getting in the way. Dan looked for young Mike and soon saw him. He was making a valiant effort to control the younger children but his loud commands and the barking and racing of a half-grown black dog which seemed to be his, were only adding to the general confusion. Dan looked about for Squatter Smith, too, but he was not in the crowd as the meeting came to order.

Dan never forgot John Worst. He wasn't a handsome man. Nowhere nearly as good looking as Pa. His straight, dark hair was parted on the side and plastered down smooth. His moustache was dark, too, and large. His forehead was high and wide, his nose straight, his ears close to his head. There were deep lines from his nose to his mouth and little lines about his eyes. He wore his glasses on a chain and as he stood talking he took them off and put them on again, peering intently at the men in front of him. He was the only man dressed in store clothes and his winged collar and black tie added to his dignity.

But the men in overalls were not afraid of him and without hesitation they were soon asking the questions that were important to them. These men had been in North Dakota longer than Dan and the neighbors in his community. They knew what they wanted; what they thought would solve their problems.

"Mr. Worst, when are we going to get state-owned grain elevators, that's what I'd like to know," one man asked. "We got county scales when you wuz in the Senate. That was a good thing. We can get honest weight on our loads now. But until we get state-owned grain elevators we'll never get honest grading of our grain, nor fair prices neither."

"How can we keep the railroad from giving free passes to the politicians?" another asked before the first question was answered. "It ain't just the fellers we send to Bismarck who gets free passes now. It's got so even out here in the counties, the men who'll vote the way Bismarck wants allus gets back in time to vote, no matter where they be."

"It ain't the way Bismarck wants 'em to vote," another voice chimed in. "It's the way Minneapolis wants 'em to vote. The seat of North Dakota government is in the Merchants Hotel in St. Paul, not in Bismarck."

The voices were growing bitter and angry.

"How can we get it so all the bankers and elevator operators and merchants in this state ain't just the underlings of the Interests?"

"Listen, Mr. Worst," one farmer demanded. "I heered that a group of men from the Red River valley got together and tried to buy a seat on the Minneapolis Chamber of Commerce.

That is where grain prices is fixed. They figgered if someone representing the farmers had a seat there'd be a chance of doing something. But someway the Chamber of Commerce got wind of it and kept the farmers off, even though they had the money. Is that true?"

"I heerd that Jim Hill come out here to a grain growers convention and told the farmers he was fer higher prices fer wheat. Told 'em he was fer wheat bringin' a dollar a bushel instead of 60¢ or 65¢ like now. Everybody knows the railroad is doing everything in their power to keep wheat prices down. Now what sort of business is that?"

John Worst let them ask their questions. Get their grievances "off their chests" as Mom would say. Some of the questions Dan had heard asked or hinted at before. The charge that the Interests owned and operated the state, against the farmers and for their own gain, was being shouted openly here, and some of the accusations were new and not too clear to Dan.

The calm authority in John Worst's voice quieted all undertones when at last he spoke.

"I think every man here knows that the College is for the farmers," he said and heads nodded in agreement. "I think you all know that I have fought for state-owned grain elevators. Forty billion dollars is invested in the farming industry of this state, but you men who produce the agricultural wealth don't have the voice you should have in governing the state."

Heads nodded in agreement.

"Two things must be done before you control your state," the college president went on. "North Dakota must have better farmers, first of all. Then North Dakota must have an agricultural statesmanship. By that I mean we must have farmers in political office, both out in the counties and in

Bismarck. Farmers have the numerical strength to control the state government, but instead of electing your own men to office, who do you send to Bismarck?"

He waited.

"Bunch of lawyers," one voice said.

"Most of us farmers ain't got the education to go to the legislature."

"There are men among you with intelligence enough," Worst insisted. "There are educated farmers in the state, too, and more of them each year. There would be more efficiency in government and a more democratic administration, and politics would be on a higher level, if you sent those men to Bismarck."

Then he turned to the problem before them that day. A State Farmers Institute Board was being planned and next year the college expected to take practical instruction in agriculture out to the farmers through those Institutes. The plans were well under way, he said. In the meantime there were summer courses at the college and extension courses. He explained them all. These were the ways by which the College was engaged in developing the agricultural statesmanship which he believed in.

It was a program Dan had never dreamed of. John Worst had knowledge of farm production and farm marketing he did not know existed. A whole new world was spread before Dan's eyes as John Worst talked. The Agriculture College became alive; its doors open and its vast funds of knowledge waiting. More than that, there would soon be help for the farmers who could not leave their work and go to Fargo. Farmers like Pa. He must find out how to get a Farmers Institute in his own county next year. He must tell Mom everything, so she could get started right away.

Dan waited as the men crowded around the college president when he had finished talking. He had no hesitancy about asking a question.

"You young farmers," John Worst said as he shook Dan's hand. "This job of working out the state's salvation is going to be up to you. Changes don't come overnight. You know that, don't you?"

Dan could only say "yes, sir," but he'd never thought of North Dakota's problems before. He had his own private fight with the Interests if the Osbornes were to make out, he knew. But it only involved getting Slim to break with them and come home. The way John Worst put it, the financial woes of all the farmers in the state seemed to land squarely on Dan's shoulders. Well, he would remember all that had been said so he could tell Mom. This was something big. Something important.

With a "Thank you, sir," Dan shook hands again and turned away from the crowd. He'd be off for home just as soon as he found someone to ask about the circuit rider. He started toward the straw stack where he had left Prince . . . and looked straight into the face of Squatter Smith. Beside him Mike Welsh, half proud, half defiant, seemed waiting for Dan to make the first move.

Dan caught his breath in surprise and managed to say "Hello."

"Why didn't you say you were coming to the meeting?" Squatter asked.

"I didn't know there was a meeting," Dan replied. "I only found out about it after I got here. When Mike told me last night."

"I guess that's right," Mike agreed.

"What did you come for, if not the meeting?"

Squatter's blue eyes were half shut but Dan felt as though this man could see into his very mind.

"To find out about getting the circuit rider to hold services in our neighborhood," Dan told him. "And I haven't done anything about it yet, either. Who'll know, anyway?" He looked from Squatter to Mike.

Squatter nodded toward the store. "Folks in there will know," he said. "Come on. I've got to get groceries. Canned milk and stuff."

Squatter listened as Dan inquired about the minister and wrote down the name and address given him. Not until then did he seem satisfied that Dan was telling the truth.

"Starting home tonight?" he asked.

"I might as well," Dan said. "I probably can find some place along the way to spend the night."

"Probably can," Squatter agreed and turned to the business of buying his supplies.

When Dan rode back from the straw stacks Squatter was mounted and waiting. He waved good bye to Mike with a friendly grin then reined his horse along side Dan's.

Dan's mind was so filled with the things he had heard that it scarcely seemed strange they should ride together in silence most of the time. He wished he could have told John Worst about Pa's part in county politics. He wished Pa could hear John Worst talk. All of the business of getting elected to office was a lot more important than Dan had ever imagined. He could see it now. Well, Pa was sure to be elected school commissioner, and Pa was an educated man. He was the kind of man John Worst had been talking about. Dan put his mind on the things he must be sure to remember and tell Mom about when he got home. She'd manage somehow to get an Institute in their part of the country next year.

11. *But Not To Stay*

DAN had so much to tell he hardly knew where to begin. Pa and Mom and the kids, and Punkin, too, all gathered around him as he sat on the steps in the cool dusk telling of his unexpected adventure. Squatter Smith seemed to interest Pa as much as John Worst himself.

"If . . . he's no great shakes as a farmer . . . did he agree with John Worst?" Pa asked.

"I couldn't quite make out," Dan admitted. "He didn't talk much until just before we turned in. I never thought he'd ask me to spend the night at his place. Gee, Pa, you should see his shanty. He's built a sod shelf about 18 inches wide and three feet high, all around the four walls inside. He must have got packing boxes from somewhere, for he's got wood on the shelf and along the wall back of it, and three sides are just lined with books. On the other side he's got his dishes and pots and pans and stuff."

"What did he say?" Pa pressed.

"He said folks forget that if it wasn't for the railroad they'd have had to get here in covered wagons," Dan recalled. "And how do people think the tools and food and all get here? How would farmers get their grain to the market in Minneapolis, or anywhere else, if it wasn't for the railroad?"

"It sounds as though he was for the railroad," Eddie piped up.

"It did for a fact," Dan admitted. "The more I think of it, the more it does sound that way. But he has such a quiet way of talking. Not excited like the rest. He said the folks who criticize Jim Hill never had to meet a payroll. I suppose he meant . . ." Dan's voice trailed off. Meeting a payroll was another expression he never had heard before.

"He meant . . . it took a lot of money . . . and scheming and figuring to get the railroad through," Pa explained. "Maybe Jim Hill . . . had debts to meet, too."

"I hope he isn't against John Worst," Dan said. "Maybe I said too much. I invited him to come see you, Pa. I told him we'd give him milk for his cats if he'd give you the loan of some of his books. I was thinking, come winter . . ."

But Pa's eyes had left Dan's face and he was looking down the road. A man was riding toward them, his mustang beating a fast clip-clop on the hard paths worn in the earth by the neighbor's wagon wheels. Punkin's ears shot up and he ran barking toward the road. The whole family was suddenly silent, waiting, almost apprehensive. This was no one from the neighborhood. They knew every horse and rider too well.

The horse swung into the path that led to the house and even in the twilight Dan knew. He sat as though paralyzed, staring, and so did Mom and the kids. But Pa was suddenly standing up. Before their eyes he took a step . . . then another.

"Slim!"

It was a choking, half-hysterical sob. Pa's hands were out and Dan jumped to his feet. Pa would fall! He couldn't walk!

But Pa was standing . . . alone . . . walking.

"Slim!"

"Pa!"

Slim was off his horse and his arms around Pa before Dan fairly was on his feet. Everyone was around them; Mom and Eddie and Grace and even Punkin who seemed to understand who he was. They were all crying and grabbing for him and repeating his name as though there wasn't anything else to say. When Dan looked at Pa there were tears streaming down his cheeks but he was so happy the tears were part of the smile.

Dan waited. Wasn't Slim even going to speak to him? He was hugging the kids and ruffling their hair and squeezing Mom and kissing her.

"Mom, you old Simon Legree!" he was saying, just like back home. "Grace, you tomboy you!"

This was Slim! And Eddie kept hugging his skinny legs and just saying "Slim! Slim!"

Wasn't he ever going to speak to Dan?

Over Mom's shoulder Slim finally met Dan's eyes and the look said clear enough that he didn't want Dan to talk.

"Dan, you young devil," was all he said but he clapped his hand on Dan's shoulder as though everything was going to be all right.

"How did you find us?" Mom was asking. Now that the first excitement was over she must know all the facts.

"I was in Minot," Slim explained. "Had to go there on a little business and I ran into a Dr. Johnson. When he learned my name *he* told me."

There was an emphasis on that word *he* which Dan knew was meant for him. He could see now that he had been wrong, back in Williston, when he hadn't followed Slim out of the restaurant; hadn't told him about Pa. Well, Slim was home now. He'd tell him as soon as they were alone. But now everyone was asking questions at once.

"What are you doing?"

"Where are you living?"

"How long have you been riding?"

"Did you have any supper?"

"What I could do to one of your meals, Mom!" Slim said. "Just anything at all, so long as you cook it."

They all piled into the kitchen then, Slim pushing Pa's chair, and as Dan lit the kerosene lamps Mom set about frying potatoes in butter and putting the coffee on to boil.

"Grace, you and Eddie go get some lettuce and green onions from the garden," Mom said but they protested, still hanging on to Slim.

"Let Dan do it," Grace wailed so Dan went out in the fading light and got a plate of garden lettuce and radishes and onions. He knew what Mom was going to fix. A fried egg salad with vinegar and salt and pepper. There wasn't any meat in the house. Mom had said they'd have to make out with partridge or quail until the Nelsons got around to butchering.

Dan didn't waste any time in the garden. He wanted to know what Slim would tell the family about himself and what he had been doing. When he got back to the kitchen, Slim was telling stories about the railroad men who worked at the round house in Williston and everyone was laughing. He'd brought a bag of hard candy for the kids and cigars for Pa, and a big gray back comb for Ma's hair.

"It isn't much," he said apologetically. "I didn't stop ten minutes after Dr. Johnson told me about Pa, and where he thought your homestead was located."

It made Dan feel mean. He should have told Slim about Pa first of all, when he had the chance in Williston. That night in Minot there'd been no time. Slim hadn't let him talk. But in Williston, well, it had been his fault there.

Dan couldn't ask Slim any questions now. He just sat and listened as Slim told them about jobs he'd had since he came to North Dakota. He didn't say much about any of them. He'd been "here and there" doing "this and that."

"I can't file on a homestead until I'm 21 you know, Pa," Slim said. "By that time all the land will be taken up, the way homesteaders are coming in this year."

"There'll be land . . . for sale," Pa explained. "There're two young Germans . . . right near here. They'd pay up and get title . . . any time they had a buyer."

Slim said it was worth looking into, but even as he said it, Dan thought he was just putting Pa off. Perhaps Pa thought so too.

"Maybe . . . you like what you're doing . . . better," Pa said. It wasn't asking Slim outright, but it was as near to it as Pa or Mom would come, Dan was sure.

"Oh, I don't know," Slim answered easily. "Now you like farming, don't you, Pa? You were always telling us about things back on the farm when I was a kid."

So Slim wasn't going to tell them what he was doing. Or whether he liked it. He looked around the room and finally spied his old guitar in its case on top of the organ. The next minute his dark head was bent over the instrument, one ear to the strings as he tuned it. He began humming and strumming chords and soon he was singing. His voice was a good, deep baritone and Dan almost forgot the hurt and misgivings that were piling up inside him as Slim sang.

> "Oh, the hinges are of leather
>   And the windows have no glass
> And the board roof lets the howling blizzard in,
>   And I hear the hungry coyote
>   As he sneaks up through the grass
> Round my little, low sod shanty, on the plain."

He winked at Grace, and the kids laughed and he strummed the strings and kept on singing until Mom finally said it was way past bedtime and they could hear Slim sing another night.

She was hoping he'd say a word about staying, Dan knew, but he didn't.

"You can sleep with Dan upstairs," Mom said. "I'll get you one of Pa's nightshirts."

"Call me in the morning and we'll see how I make out with the cows," Slim said cheerfully as he kissed them good night. Then he stood gripping Pa's shoulder and shaking his head a little, before he left them.

"Come on, kids. Upstairs to bed!"

Eddie and Grace raced to the stairs when he spoke instead of protesting and lagging back, as usual. Dan wished he could stop for just one minute with Mom before he went upstairs. His throat got tight at the thought of being alone with Slim. What was Slim going to say to him?

He found out as soon as the bedroom door was shut.

"Why didn't you tell me?" Slim demanded. The smiles were gone now and in the lamp light his face was set and white and the little black moustache was just a straight, hard line.

"You didn't give me much chance," Dan said. "I intended to. That's what I went to Williston for. I didn't have any chance that time in Minot."

"You had plenty of chance in Williston," Slim said. "I could have gotten away easier then than now."

Perhaps it was because he was speaking low, not to be overheard, but there was a strained note in Slim's voice. A worried undertone.

"O.K. Slim, it was my fault," Dan said miserably. "You didn't know. I should have made you listen."

" 'Made me listen!' All you had to do was tell me." Slim's voice was hard. "You had plenty else to say."

Dan sat down on the bed and took off his shoes. Slim was home at last, but what a wretched homecoming this was. All that gaiety and singing downstairs. Just another front. A cheerfulness Slim had put on for Pa and Mom and the kids. He wasn't going to stay. There were things he wasn't telling, too. Well, Dan wouldn't ask any questions. Silently he undressed and got into bed, turning his back toward Slim who stood at the window staring out into the night, Pa's nightshirt on his arm.

Dan didn't know when he fell asleep nor how long he had been sleeping when Slim wakened him.

"Dan," he whispered. "Come. Get up!"

Something in Slim's voice startled Dan into instant clearheadedness.

"Come," Slim said and walked cautiously to the window.

The bare boards of the bedroom floor were cold under Dan's feet. Standing before the window he peered out into the white moonlight to see two figures in the road in front of their house. They seemed to be looking for something in the grass and when they stood up Dan recognized them at once. It was Ike Sheets and Tom.

"Well, I'll . . ." Dan left the sentence unfinished.

"Do you know them?"

"Yes, they're neighbors," Dan said. "And the old man's no good. He fought Pa in two elections this spring, Slim. Whatever he's up to, it's for no good."

"He fought Pa?" Slim asked and in the darkness his voice seemed to reach across the breach that had separated him from Dan. "How do you mean, Red?"

"He fixed one election in advance so Pa couldn't do anything," Dan explained. "Then he tried to keep Pa from getting nominated for school commissioner in the primary this month. But Pa won!"

Dan wanted to tell Slim all about the election and the fight, but this wasn't the time to do it.

"What deviltry do you suppose he's up to now?" Dan asked.

"It looks like he's pacing off Pa's homestead," Slim replied. "I saw the two of them coming down the road. Is that the end of Pa's land, where they're standing?"

Dan peered out into the moonlight again.

"If it is, then our house isn't even on our land," Dan said. "Look where they are."

"Didn't you measure it off when you got here?"

Dan shook his head as he recalled the day they had found their claims. "We started from the north line stake," Dan told him. "Everybody was so excited about the willows because there'd be water there. When they said the trees were on our land . . ."

"Didn't you even look for the stake?"

Dan had looked as he drove along from the south end of Ike's claim, but when the Nelsons had said the trees were his,

Dan had just accepted it. Then the Nelsons had gone on, looking for the next stake and had found it at the south end of their quarter section. Well he remembered it all now.

"Our house must be on the Nelsons' land," Dan said. "Luckily for us they're our friends. One way or another, Ike Sheets has been fighting us ever since we got to North Dakota."

"Friends or enemies won't make any difference with the Land Office, Red," Slim warned. "You have to comply with the homestead laws, and the law says you build a house on your land and live in it, six months out of every year. That doesn't mean on the neighbor's land, or anywhere else."

Dan didn't know what to say. It was humiliating to have Slim find out about a mistake like this. If Pa hadn't complied with the law it was Dan's fault and he knew it. But even as his cheeks grew hot with mortification, he knew that Slim was going to stand by the family in this new trouble. Slim would know what to do.

"Look," Slim said quietly. "They're measuring it off all right. They're checking back on their tracks."

In the white light Dan could see Ike Sheets walk slowly a few paces and wait until Tom came to him before he walked ahead again.

"They've got a rope or measuring line of some sort," Slim explained. "You know what that fellow's likely figuring on, don't you?"

Dan didn't answer. Ike was figuring on making trouble some way, but he didn't know how, and sensing it, Slim gave the explanation.

"When Pa goes to prove up he'll contest it," Slim said. "At least that's what it looks like to me. He might try to get the farm away from Pa. Lucky for us I couldn't sleep."

Us. Never had a word sounded so good. *Us.* Dan could have grabbed Slim and pounded him for joy. He wanted to say something about Slim's sleeplessness. That maybe he'd sleep better now that he was home. But he felt choked and couldn't think of what to say. So he stood by the open window shivering with anxiety and nervousness and uncertain happiness as well as the chill of the night.

"We'll have to move the house if that's really the end of our land," Dan finally managed to whisper between chattering teeth.

Slim turned back to the bed. "Soon as it's daylight you and I'd better slip out and do some measuring ourselves," he said. "It isn't likely those two will be up at the crack of dawn. Not after their night prowling tonight."

Dan didn't sleep after that. It was lucky indeed that Slim had come home this particular night and that something had kept him from sleeping. Ike Sheets wasn't going to take his defeat at the polls without striking back at Pa, that was clear. He'd won on all counts when the county got organized, but the election had shown him up in a bad light in front of everybody.

Dan wondered, as he lay waiting for daylight, how Tom felt about this last trickery. He hadn't seen Tom since before the election. Not since the fire and the barn-raising, in fact. Everybody'd been singing his praises then, and Mom had always been good to him. But it didn't make much difference how Tom felt; he'd have to do as his old man said. Once before he'd tried to make things right by riding to Williston to fetch Dan home. Would he try to find some way to undo what Ike was plotting now? Well, it wouldn't be necessary this time. Slim had caught Ike in the act, and the Osbornes would get out of their difficulty themselves.

With the first streak of light Slim and Dan slipped out of the house, got a measuring line, and searched the road at the place where Ike and Tom had been standing. There wasn't a sign of a surveyor's mark, nor any indication that one had been removed.

"I can find the stake at the north end of our land," Dan said. "If they haven't moved it, that is. They must have started measuring from something."

"Let's get a move on, then."

Slim didn't talk as they hurried along the trail but it was like old times, this doing a job together and Dan felt good all through. It was all right if Slim didn't want to talk. Just so long as he didn't hold a grudge against Dan.

The marker was still in its place and when the measuring was finished it was clear that the house was just across the line on the Nelsons' land. Slim shook his head as he rolled up the rope and started for the kitchen where Mom was busy getting breakfast.

"What have you two been up to?" Mom asked. She'd put her front hair up on curlers again, Dan noticed. Prettied up for Slim.

Slim let Dan tell what had happened and he didn't say a word about Dan's failure to measure off the land as he should have done in the beginning. Pa looked serious as he heard the story, but Mom wasn't disturbed at all.

"It's only been a little more than three months since we built," she said. "We'll move the house to where it should be and live on our own land more than the law requires. But it was Providence that you came home last night, Slim. The Lord has had his arms around all of us."

"Moving the house isn't so simple, Mom," Dan said slowly. "How are we going to do it?"

"I've seen them moving houses back in Cincinnati," Mom announced, business-like. "You ride over to the Nelsons right after breakfast. Mr. Nelson'll know how. You'll have to get Ernst and Peter, too. I wish we could ask Jim Jackson, but we can't. Let's see now, what can I scare up to feed them. We've got to do it right away."

"She's right," Pa agreed. He was standing up alone by his chair, but no one mentioned it, although Dan could scarcely take his eyes from the spot. "We'll do it . . . tomorrow. The sooner . . . the better."

Dan wondered if Pa and Mom were thinking it would be well to do the moving while Slim was there, so two Osbornes would be able to help with the work. Always in the past the neighbors had done more than their share because Dan was the only one to help; the only one to work in repayment. But if Slim were staying . . . He'd see how badly they needed him if he stayed only a day or two.

Mr. Nelson knew how to move the house. Knew it would take manpower to do it too, so Dan rode on for Ernst and Peter after telling the Nelsons there'd be a surprise for them at his house. He didn't tell them Slim had come home. They'd ask questions he couldn't answer very well. Better to let Slim do his own talking.

Petra was helping Mom when Dan returned, her cheeks flushed and pretty as she bent over the big iron kettle on the kitchen stove.

"Goldie Locks has been whipping up fried cakes all afternoon," Slim said as Dan came in. "She gave me all the holes. Look what she's got me doing now!"

He held up the potato he was peeling. "Only other girl I'd peel potatoes for is Mom."

—156—

"Petra's too little for you, Slim," Eddie announced gravely. "She's Dan's girl."

"You've got things all figured out, haven't you, old wise-acres," Slim said good-naturedly as Petra turned her back to both of them and embarrassment flushed Dan's cheeks. "Now who's your girl, I'd like to know."

Grace giggled but Eddie wasn't the least disturbed.

"I'm going to get a girl for myself," Eddie said. "I'm going way off and get her and she'll be real beautiful."

Then Mom ordered them all out of the kitchen. "Eddie, sometimes I wonder . . ." she said. "Go help Dan with the work and stop your dreaming."

There was plenty to do before the men came the next morning. It was a joy to see Pa standing on his two feet that day and introducing Slim, with a proud look on his face.

"My son, C. E. Junior," he said as Slim shook hands with each man in turn. "He just recently found out . . . where we were located . . . What with his moving around and us leaving Cincinnati . . . we sort of lost track of each other . . . for a little spell."

It had been quite a little spell, but Pa and Mom weren't going to admit it to the neighbors and Slim carried on just as they'd wish him to do.

"You got a homestead?" Chris asked at once. He was excited and eager to get at their new job, and curious about Slim too.

"By the time Uncle Sam lets me file on a homestead there won't be any free land left," Slim answered. "But I might work out a business deal and buy one. Pa and I've been talking about it."

Dan wondered if they'd talked about it while he was gone

yesterday, but he didn't ask the question. Chris, however, was all curiosity.

"Are you going to stay with your folks now?" he asked and Dan held his breath waiting for Slim's reply.

"Well, I haven't asked Mom how long she can stand me under foot," he said easily. "Maybe she can put up with me for a week or so."

A week or so . . .

Dan couldn't look at either Pa or Mom.

A week or so . . .

It was just as well Chris went on talking.

"Gee, I wish you'd stay long enough to go haying with us," he said. "Soon as the grass is ready we'll all go down south of here and put up hay for the stock this winter. I'll bet Dan would appreciate having someone to help him for once. Not that Nels and I won't help him again."

Dan saw Slim straighten up and stare hard at Chris. Slim hadn't realized how dependent the Osbornes were on the neighbors, of course. Dan's own cheeks burned at the thought of it, although he knew Chris meant no unkindness.

"When will you start haying?" Slim asked.

"About another week, I guess. We were going to ride down tomorrow and see how it looks and stake out our plots. With so much of the prairie burnt over, there may be more folks counting on that strip of grass we saved than we know about."

Then they told Slim about the horse thieves and the prairie fire and praised Dan for his part. He was glad then that no one except Mom and Pa knew why he had followed the outlaws.

Talk was cut short when Mr. Nelson took charge of the moving. With crowbars the house was lifted onto planks that could be chained together to form a stoneboat. It was slow, heavy work, taking all the strength of all of them. Once the planks were secured it was easy enough for the horses to move the house to the Osborne land. Then the planks had to be removed, just as carefully as they'd been slid under the building. It was a long, hard job with every man working every minute, but as soon as the stove was up again, Mom and Petra whipped up a meal that was worth it. Sour cream pancakes and maple syrup. Fried potatoes and scrambled eggs. Coffee and the fried cakes Petra had made the day before. And Slim helped, flipping the pancakes over and bringing big platters of food to the table and joking with everyone.

"I wonder what Ike Sheets thinks now," Chris laughed, pushing his chair back from the table. "He must have seen what's been going on."

Dan had been thinking about Ike too, and so had Pa.

"I wonder what he'll try next," Pa said as he walked cautiously from the table to the window to look out toward the Sheets shack.

"Maybe he'll go set fire to our hay," Chris suggested. "We'd better stake out our plots right away." Then he turned to Slim. "Want to ride along?"

"Say when," Slim replied.

Dan had to keep reminding himself in the days that followed that Slim really wasn't going to stay home. Nels and Chris, Slim and himself riding together, hunting together. Nels with his accordion and Slim with the guitar, playing and singing as they sat around their camp fire at night. This was the way it ought to be. They talked of the work ahead, and harvesting problems. Slim knew a lot about farming; how much binder twine to buy, how many grain bags they'd need. He looked serious when they talked about threshing and sometimes he didn't have his mind on what the others were saying.

They were a long way from home, jogging along in the late afternoon sunshine, when Dan sensed that something had happened while they were gone. He was the first to spot two grays among the horses and cows pastured beyond the Osborne barn. He didn't say anything until he had parted with the Nelsons. Then Slim, too, saw the gray horses.

"What do you suppose is up, Red?" Slim asked.

"I hate to say what I've been thinking," Dan admitted. "Mom just might have gone to Minot while we were away. I'd figured I'd get along someway. Dicker with Ernst and Peter for a hand at harvest and the use of their two horses, maybe."

The relaxed look had left Slim's face and he gave his mustang a quick kick. "She hasn't got the money, has she?" Slim asked.

"About enough for the machines we've got to have," Dan said. "That's all."

But Mom had bought everything. Shining with newness were a mowing machine, hay rack, horse rake, and harvester. Dan and Slim pulled up in front of the row of clean machines, bright with red paint and gleaming metal. They were still sitting there when Mom came bustling out, smiling and happy.

"We're all fixed now," she said gesturing toward her purchases and looking beyond them to the fine, broad-breasted horses staked out where the grass was greenest near the well.

When neither Slim nor Dan spoke, Mom turned to them quickly.

"What's the matter?" she asked. "I thought you two'd be pleased as punch. Those two greys aren't more than 3 or 4 years old and I got them for $135 each."

"With what money?" Slim asked.

Mom's face clouded.

"We had to have them," she announced positively. "I'd thought we might get Ernst and Peter to help with harvesting but I talked to them the day we moved the house." She was shaking her head slowly. "They'll both be gone by harvest. They've got jobs with a threshing crew first, and as soon as threshing season's over they're going to work in the logging camps. I got them to help me bring the machines out from Minot, but that's all we can count on them for. And we had to have the horses."

"Look, Mom, let's get down to cases," Slim said quietly as he slid from his horse and began to unfasten the venison he had brought back. "You paid $125 for that harvester. And $50 more for the mowing machine and $25 for the horse rake and another $25 for the hay rack, and $135 for each of the horses, you say. Not to mention the other little stuff. There's more than $500 spread out in the barnyard, isn't there?"

"Yes, Slim," Mom admitted. "But I only had to borrow half."

"Have you figured what you're likely to get from the crops this year? Keeping out seed for next spring? And paying off this debt?"

Slim wasn't looking at Mom. He was unfastening the saddle, fussing with the horse, avoiding her eyes.

"I know we're just barely going to make out to eat," Mom admitted and her voice was husky and not much more than a whisper. "But if we get our land broke this fall, and harrowed and ready for cultivating next spring, we've got to put two teams to plowing. We've got to start just as soon as haying's done, and again when harvest's over. If we don't, it'll be just the same next year. We can't have idle land."

"You're figuring on paying off that debt this fall? And not borrowing more?"

"We'll pay it off with the first grain we sell," Mom said positively. "The interest's too high to be carrying it a minute longer than need be. I see that, all right."

She sounded a little annoyed. Or maybe worried. Slim sensed it too.

"I guess you've got everything figured out," he said and depositing the vension on the back steps he took his horse to the well.

Dan stood with Mom for a moment as Prince pulled at the bridle. Had she been counting on Slim to help with the work? All that plowing? Was that why she had bought the fine team and the new machines? The Osbornes would be fixed as well as anyone in the neighborhood when it was all paid for. Another year, if only he'd stay . . .

"Mom," Dan began, but she turned away from him and went into the house, so Dan followed Slim to the well to water Prince.

"Some patches of that hay were ready to cut, Red," Slim said without looking up at him. "We'd better get at it right away. Tomorrow."

But the joy was gone. Slim's face was serious and he couldn't joke much at supper although he tried. The next morning he and Dan left for the hay field, to work for days in the burning sun from the first streak of light until dusk hid the rows of drying grass.

No time to talk then. The click-clock of the saw-tooth knives beat endlessly in Dan's ears. The sun scorched his hands and face and sent sweat rolling down his body. Flies and mosquitoes drove men and horses furious. They ate and slept between smudge fires of smouldering sage weed. Beyond the pungent smoke, zinging swarms of black insects hovered waiting to torture them.

"Oh, for a good high wind," Dan groaned as he started the fires and prepared breakfast one morning near the end of the week. "It might drive these pests off. Thank Heaven we're almost through."

But he sensed as he said it that no one was listening and he looked up to see Slim intently watching two teams that were coming into the hay field. Even in the hazy sunrise Dan recognized the drivers.

"Why, that's Isaiah Parker and his wife," Dan exclaimed. "Gosh, is she going to work here? In this blistering heat?"

Slim didn't answer. As Mr. Parker came toward them he began adjusting the fly nets that protected the horses, his back to Dan and the newcomers. And Dan, standing by his camp fire, realized that Mr. Parker was looking beyond him; looking at Slim even when he spoke.

"You've got a head start, I see," he said.

"We ought to finish up this week," Dan agreed. "We're all done except loading and taking it back home." He felt uncomfortable. Slim and Mr. Parker . . . Did they know each other? Slim had known about the sheep, somehow.

"Two of you been workin'?" Mr. Parker asked still looking at Slim.

"Yes," Dan answered. "This is my brother, Slim."

Slim turned slowly then, his eyes on Mr. Parker's face. One arm lay along the neck of the big gray gelding Mom had bought and he leaned against the animal just as he had leaned against the doorway between the bar and the gambling room back in Williston. Self-possessed, defiant, hard.

"We've met before," Slim said and his voice was like back in Williston too. "I'm right glad Mr. Parker got here today.

I know he'll be glad to help load the hay and take it back to Pa's place."

"What?" Dan gasped. "Mr. Parker came to . . ."

"Mr. Parker won't mind giving you a hand, Red," Dan heard Slim saying, slow and insolent like. "I'm over-due back in Williston already. I'm awful glad he's here to help you."

Speechless, Dan stared at Slim and then at Mr. Parker. What was the man going to say? What was he going to do? When he didn't speak up, Dan turned to Slim again. But Slim had left the work horses and was saddling his own mustang with quick, certain moves. In another minute he had mounted and was riding over to the camp fire. He wheeled his horse so his back was toward Mr. Parker.

"It's better this way, Red," he said and he tried to smile a little, but it wasn't right. Everything was wrong again and there was no way of finding out why. No time to say anything.

"I'll be seeing you." Then the mustang was galloping off across the prairie toward Williston.

12. *Another Candidate*

DAN stared in speechless disbelief as Slim rode away. How could his brother leave him like this? What was he to say to Mom and Pa? They were expecting Slim back. Counting on him for help too, although they should have known better.

It wasn't the work that worried Dan, though. He and Mom had managed to get the crops in last spring. They could turn to now and start plowing, and harvest the crop, and plow again if the snow held off. They'd get most of the land cropped next season if it killed them! It was the certainty that something was wrong, or Slim wouldn't have left like this. There was everything to keep him home. Even a chance to buy a piece of land for himself when Ernst and Peter were ready to sell.

And the way he had talked to Mr. Parker! Just because the man had brought sheep into grain country when the Interests didn't want him to. Suppose they did own the gambling hall in Williston where Slim worked. Or was there more to it than that?

Miserably Dan turned to face Mr. Parker.

"Slim didn't mean it the way it sounded," he tried to explain. "He'd been away from his job longer than he expected."

Mr. Parker looked as though he didn't believe it. "I'll help you. Today," he said.

Today. Well, one day's help was better than none, and Dan had helped Mr. Parker more than once. In silence they piled the hay on Dan's rack; uncomfortably they said "So long" when they parted.

All the way home Dan tried to think of how he would tell Mom and Pa that Slim had gone. How could he explain it? What was he to say to Mom? And to Pa?

The more Dan thought about Pa, the easier it became, somehow. Slim had been closer to Pa than anyone. Maybe Slim had explained things to Pa. Maybe Pa would understand. It wasn't natural for Dan to go to Pa with anything but with Slim it was different. If Slim had talked to anyone, it would have been Pa.

Dan started looking for his father as soon as he neared the house. Mom and Eddie and Grace would all come running to meet him, he knew. If he could just get away from them for a few minutes, to talk to Pa alone.

But he couldn't. For sitting in the shade with Pa and Mom and the kids, was Squatter Smith.

"Dan," Mom called. "We've got company. Let the horses cool off before you water them." And she motioned to him to join them.

"I took you up," Squatter said as Dan approached. "Thought I'd like to make your folks' acquaintance."

"He brought good news and bad too," Mom said.

"Now don't say that," Pa said quietly. "It's all right."

But Dan knew it wasn't.

"What is it?" he asked.

"First off, there's going to be a circuit rider coming out from Minot, so we can count on services in another month," Mom said. Then, drawing a long breath, "Ike Sheets has been up to some more of his politics."

Mom looked across the fields to the Sheets shanty as though she expected to see Ike coming any minute.

"He's got a man running against your father on the Democratic ticket," Squatter explained.

"But how could he?" Dan asked. "Ike's a Republican too. Anybody'd think he's running both parties."

Dan was hot and tired and too disturbed to try to reason it out. But somehow Ike Sheets was making more trouble.

"He must be pretty wily," Squatter said. "He came over into the east end of the county and got the most popular man there to say he'd run on the Democratic ticket. He's got them convinced they'll not get a school in their end of the county if your father's elected."

Dan sighed wearily and sat down in the grass.

"As a matter of fact, I had no intention of coming this far when I started out, Red," Squatter went on. "I just went to a neighbor's place to get some milk, and found out what was being said against your Pa. He's got some tough opposition now."

"Who is this Democrat?" Dan asked.

"Name of Anderson," Squatter said. "He's a great big, handsome Norwegian and everybody likes him. Gets along well with everyone. He'll pull a lot of votes."

"Mr. Smith says he has a big family and that all the

Norwegians in that part of the county have big families too," Mom added and she looked glum.

"There's another thing," Squatter said rubbing his hands over his long, black beard. "They've got fifteen children or more in that neighborhood and Anderson tells me the state school fund is apportioned according to the number of children in a school district. So his end of the county could get more state money to help out with a school than yours. Unless there are more here to make up a school district, that is."

Mom sighed and shook her head. There weren't fifteen children in the west end of the county, all told.

"If there are more children over East . . . they should get the first school," Pa spoke up. "I'd favor that . . . if we can't get two schools."

"But Pa!" Mom protested. "Eddie and Grace?"

"Eddie and Grace might have to . . . go over there at first," Pa said.

"You mean it?" Squatter turned away from Mom and Dan and looked straight at Pa. "You mean if you were elected you'd start a school over East first?"

"Certainly," Pa said and there was no doubt that he meant it. "The county school commissioner represents . . . the whole county. He's supposed to organize districts . . . where the children are."

Squatter whistled a long, low whistle.

"What's the matter?" Dan asked. "Isn't Pa right?"

"Sure he's right," Squatter said. "But that's not the way the folks over East have been told. This fellow Sheets has got them all thinking they'll never get a school if Osborne's elected. That all he intends to do is get a school for his own kids. So they're all going to vote the other ticket."

"All the men with families and all the Norwegians," Mom

groaned. "And there's a regular Norwegian settlement over there."

As far as Dan was concerned it might have been all right, except that he recalled the things John Worst had said about the man who should hold political office. That and the primary election day.

"The first political job John Worst ever had was county superintendent of schools, wasn't it?" he asked, scarce expecting anyone to answer.

"You and I are thinking the same thing," Squatter said nodding his black head over and over again.

"What's that?" Pa asked.

Squatter hesitated before he began explaining it.

"It's more than just this election," he said. "It's getting the right men into all political offices for the good of the state. You start by holding some small county office, then you go on to the legislature. North Dakota's got to have the farm interests in Bismarck pretty soon."

"This Anderson sounds . . . like a good man," Pa said.

"He's a good man all right," Squatter agreed. "That's where this Sheets was so smart. But Anderson hasn't the education or the intelligence to go on. Given your health back, you have."

"Go on?" Pa repeated. "No, I'd not go on as you say . . . All I hoped to do was see that we got schools started. Somebody . . . has to do it and it's something . . . I could do."

But Squatter was just sitting there looking off toward the horizon and nodding his head over and over again.

"If the folks over East knew how you stand, they'd elect you," he said finally. "They've heard John Worst and his ideas about the kind of men who should represent the farming interests. If they were assured . . ."

He left the sentence unfinished, but they all knew what he meant.

"There's got to be some way to let them know, then," Mom said. "Somebody's got to tell them. If Pa was elected he'd do as he says. If they should have the first school, he'd get it for them. But he'd get us a school the next year, wouldn't you, Pa?"

She'd gotten to her feet and was standing over them, her hands on her hips and her face set.

"Now don't get yourself . . . all upset, Mom," Pa said quietly. "Anderson'll do the same thing. Dan, what about watering the horses? Where's Slim?"

Pa had gotten up from his chair and was walking a little.

Dan couldn't tell them then. He was sick with dread again at the thought of it. Pa might not take it so easily. You couldn't tell how he'd take it.

"He didn't come, this load," Dan said and started toward the team.

Mechanically he unhitched the horses. He'd unload the hay close by the barn so it would be handy for winter and pro- tected from the wind, too. But when he got back from the well Pa was waiting for him. While Mom was talking politics with Squatter, he'd wheeled himself out to the hayrack.

"Is everything all right, Dan?" he asked.

Dan started to say yes, but it was no good. He had to tell Pa. This was what he'd wanted, a chance to talk to Pa alone. So he pushed the wheel chair around behind the load of hay where Mom couldn't see them.

"Pa, did Slim say anything to you?" Dan asked. "Anything he didn't tell the rest of us?"

Pa didn't answer at once.

"He didn't tell me enough, Dan," he said at last. "He . . . said he'd work things out as soon as he could."

"But he didn't tell you what it was? I mean . . . Pa, did you get the idea he's working for the Interests some way? Against the farmers? Against people like us?"

"No. No, I don't think that's what's wrong."

So Pa, too, knew that something was wrong.

"Then what is it?" Dan almost pleaded. "Pa, do you know I saw Slim twice before he came home?"

The look of surprise on Pa's face was answer enough. Slim hadn't told him and now Dan had to. There was little enough to tell though, now that Dan at last let Pa know all that had happened. It wasn't much of a surprise to Pa to know that Slim had gone back to Williston.

"Up to now, Pa, I always had a feeling that if I could just talk to Slim and let him know everything, that he'd come home," Dan finally said. "But now . . . well, it's as though everything was all over. I can't go to Williston for him again. There's nothing more to tell him. He knows everything. There's nothing to go for."

"It seems that way," Pa admitted. "I wish he'd been willing to tell us more. No matter what trouble he's in."

"It didn't really seem like he was in trouble when I saw him in Williston," Dan said thoughtfully. "It was just . . . the Interests, somehow."

"Slim doesn't show how he feels," Pa said slowly. "He tries to hide it, and lets it eat away down inside."

The words, and the way Pa said them, were like a stinging blow to Dan. That was how Pa was too, and for the first time Dan sensed it. This wheel chair, not being able to walk much, not being able to take care of his family like other men . . . that was eating away inside Pa. He'd said the election didn't matter, but it did. What was it he had said? "It's something I could do." Dan heard him saying it again and he choked at the memory. Getting schools started would have meant something to the whole county and Pa could have done it. Now even that was about to be taken away from him.

Dan blinked hard as he gripped the back of the wheel chair. He'd have to do something. He'd have to talk to Squatter Smith. Surely Squatter could do something. They'd have to find a way to let the people off East know. Dan thought of Mr. Nelson. He was a Norwegian. They'd listen to him. Only how was he or anyone going to do any explaining now, with haying to be done and plowing and harvest work?

"Oh, Pa," Dan groaned. "Why did Slim have to leave us now? If he'd only stayed just a little longer."

"I know," Pa said. "But we've got to believe in him. Maybe we could help if we only knew everything. Maybe that Mr. Parker knows more than he's told you."

They were interrupted then by Squatter Smith, whistling softly as he limped toward the hay rack.

"I'm not much of a farmer," he said, "but I'll give you a hand at unloading the hay, Red. Your Mother's promised me milk for my cats, often as I want to come for it. Seems like I ought to do something in return."

He climbed onto the bulging load and began pitching the hay down into a pile beside the barn. As soon as Pa had started wheeling himself back to the house Squatter slackened his efforts, however. He leaned on the pitchfork and spoke to Dan in a quiet voice.

"Red, something's got to be done about getting your Pa elected," he said. "Isn't there someone who can campaign for him? What about this brother of yours?"

Dan didn't want to talk about Slim. "He was only here for a visit," he explained. "He had to go back to his job."

"But he didn't know about Anderson when he left," Squatter persisted. "Your folks thought your Pa was as good as elected until I told them different."

"Slim couldn't do it," Dan said avoiding Squatter's eyes. "He's all tied up in some business deal. He couldn't even stay to help me finish with the haying."

"And you're the only one there is to do the farm work," Squatter said, more to himself than to Dan.

It sounded hopeless, but the memory of Pa's face as he talked about Slim was not to be forgotten.

"How soon has this campaigning got to be done?" Dan asked. "Would there be time if I could get away after harvest?"

"That's pretty late, but if he can carry his end of the county it would only take a few more votes."

"Would you help?" Dan asked. "I wouldn't even know how to start."

But Squatter didn't promise.

13. *Ruin*

AFTER haying came the plowing. It wasn't as easy as in the spring when the land was soft from the moisture of winter snows. Each day Dan watched the blue horizon for thunderheads that might bring rain, but the cobalt sky was cloudless and the sun hot. The green stalks of wheat were shading yellow, and yellow the tufts of goldenrod he turned under with the furrows.

How hard and dry the sod. How long these rows. Eighty acres stretched ahead of him, flat and gray and unyielding. If it would only rain. Never could he get the land broken before harvest. After harvest there might still be time before November came bringing snow. November and the election. After harvest he'd have to take the time to campaign for Pa, whether the plowing was finished or not.

Squatter Smith had been back twice for milk.

"There isn't much you can do now, Red," he'd said. "They're working as hard over East as you are here. They've no time for talking. They wouldn't listen to you now. Maybe after harvest, like you thought at first . . ."

But he hadn't promised any help. Just brought news from off East and took his milk and went home.

The sun grew hotter and the days shorter and burning winds blew clouds of dust into the air from the freshly turned earth. Before Dan's eyes the prairie swayed and the field of wheat was a streak of molten brass, moving in long billows before the ceaseless wind. Dirt filled Dan's nostrils and caked around his nose and mouth and eyes.

If it would only rain!

But no rain came and one morning as Dan looked across the fields toward the neighboring homesteads he saw that Jim Jackson was cutting his grain. To the south the Nelsons were still working on the unbroken land.

Dan took a few spears to the house for Pa to examine.

"I think it's too soon," Pa said. "Give it a couple more days. Maybe Jim got his crop in a little earlier. You have to allow 90 to 100 days for wheat to mature."

So Dan went back to plowing and the wheat glistened in the sun until one morning he hitched the horses to the bright new harvester, threaded the binder twine, and drove into his sea of gold, with Mom and Eddie and Grace all ready to shock, and Pa to show them how.

There was music in the sound of the fanning slats which slapped the grain down onto the machine, and in the click-clack of the knives that cut it. Dan could have sung out for joy as he drove down the first row, leaving a straight sweep of shining stubble behind him and rows of even bundles, each tied securely by the magic of the harvester. A miracle it was,

-175-

this machine that worked so smoothly. Slap! Slap! and the slats measured off the grain and bent it over. Click-clock and the knives cut it off. With a heart-warming rustle it moved across the bottom of the reaper.

"I take two bundles and prop them up against each other like so, don't I, Pa?" Mom asked.

"And we bring more," Eddie shouted, reaching after the grain. They stacked a dozen bundles together to form a circular shock, with one bundle slapped down on top, grain heads down, so the straw would protect the grain beneath it.

The work moved fast. This was more like it. Soon Dan was coming down the second row. This was what he had waited for. This and the day when he would drive the first load of grain to the elevator in Minot.

Dan had started his third row when he saw the threshing crew moving onto Jim Jackson's land. The big, red machine was followed by two wagons that looked like box cars, and behind them half a dozen hay racks with two or three men riding in each rig. Cook car and bunk car, that explained the big wagons Dan knew, for Chris and Nels had described them to him. He drew his horses to a halt and stared at the threshing outfit. Here it was in their neighborhood, and neither he nor the Nelsons were finished with harvesting! Had Jim Jackson found out, somehow, when they would be here? No wonder he'd started harvesting ahead of the others if he did. Maybe his grain wasn't ripe enough though. How would it grade if it was too green?

As Dan stared at the crew Pa came to him slowly, leaning on a cane he had fashioned from left-over lumber. He could walk pretty well now, with the support it gave.

"Tonight you go over," Pa said. "Inquire if they'll wait over . . . a day or two. Or if they're going to swing back."

"I will, Pa," Dan said as he pulled up the slackened reins and reached for the whip. "No time to lose now."

One flip at their flanks and the horses were moving again. "I'll bring lunch out to the field," Pa called after him.

They worked until Dan could no longer see the edge of the standing grain ahead of him, then Mom took the seat on the harvester and rode home while Dan walked beside her.

"Guess my muscles got softened up this summer," was all she said as she slumped in the seat.

Dan didn't wait long after he'd finshed eating. All day he'd heard the steady roar of the threshing machine on Jim Jackson's land. He'd seen the mound of tawny straw rising higher each time he'd reached the far end of the wheat field. Mounting Prince, he hurried along the road in the darkness. There was a camp fire in the Jackson yard and as he neared it he could hear the strumming of a guitar and men's voices singing.

There was a guitar back at his place, too, but no sense in thinking about that now.

In the flickering light Dan recognized Jim at once, and Tom Sheets. Ike wasn't there, nor were all of the men Dan had seen driving into Jim's yard that morning. He could guess where they were, all right. Sharing a jug at Ike's shanty no doubt. Not once had he seen Ike or Tom or Jim either since the day of the election, except the night Slim and he had watched Ike and Tom measuring off Pa's land. They must have seen the Osborne house being moved, but none had been near to say a word about it.

Dan dismounted and walked over to Jim.

"I see you're threshing," he said.

"Yes. This here crew come along and I was ready." Jim sounded friendly enough.

"How soon will you be finished?"

"Some time tomorrow, I figger."

"Who's the boss?" Dan asked looking at the strange faces before him. One man spoke up.

"I was wondering where you're going from Jim's place," Dan said. "We aren't quite ready but we've got to be threshed of course."

"We'll swing along east," the man said. "Farmers who got their grain in earlier than you folks are ready now. Farther away from Minot we go, the later folks got started planting, it seems like."

"Are you coming back this way?" Dan asked.

The man shook his head.

"We got all the business lined up that we can take care of. But there'll be other crews along. I heered there's two or three outfits working this way out of Williston."

Tom spoke up then for the first time.

"No need for you or the Nelsons to worry," he said. "There's plenty of time."

Dan didn't know much about harvesting and threshing and when Jim asked him to "set a spell" he joined the men, asking questions and getting news of the harvest.

"It's been a good year all through here they tell me," Jim volunteered.

"Wheat otta grade good," one of the men said but it seemed to Dan there was more doubt than assurance in his voice.

"You take your pay in grain?" Dan asked.

"How else?" the boss asked and laughed a little as he said it. "I never seen a farmer yet who could pay any other way."

"I guess you're right," Dan admitted. He was sure the Osbornes couldn't. Part of their grain to the threshers for their work, he was thinking. Part for seed next spring. How much would be left to sell?

"What's your land been yielding, Jim?" Dan asked.

"Fifteen bushel to the acre," Jim said.

Dan didn't like the sound of his voice nor the figure either.

"I thought North Dakota land yielded eighteen to twenty," Dan said.

The threshing boss laughed again, a mirthless "Ha-ha."

"That's what Jim Hill advertised to get you fellers out here," he said. "I ain't seen many yields like that. Ten to twelve bushel is more like it."

Ten . . .

Seventy-five acres Dan had planted to wheat, the rest to oats for winter feed. Seven hundred and fifty bushels with part of it taken by the threshers. But his yield might be better than ten to the acre. Jim had said fifteen. If he had only 700 bushels left and it sold at 65¢ that would bring only $455 and Mom owed the Interests $250.

Numbly Dan got to his feet. Their land ought to yield better than ten. Fifteen, Mom had guessed. But the way Jim Jackson had said "fifteen," Dan didn't believe it.

"Guess we'll have to wait for the next threshing crew," Dan said. "I wonder where Prince ambled off to."

He turned away from Jim and the threshers and walked to the shadow that he knew was Prince. Tom was standing beside his horse, stroking it easily.

"How you folks been?" Tom asked, self-consciously.

"All right," Dan mumbled. "Working hard."

"I found something the other day I thought the kids would like," Tom said and extended his hand toward Dan. "Just pebbles, but they'll write. Colored, like chalk."

Dan was surprised but he opened his hand and the clay-like bits rolled into his palm.

"Green and yellow and reddish," Tom was saying. "I thought of Eddie right away."

"He'll like them," Dan said as he put the pebbles in his pocket. In spite of his new worry, he was sorry for Tom. Probably he'd been lonesome with no one around except his old man. And no good meals like Mom cooked unless Mrs. Jackson fed him now and then. She hadn't been anywhere in sight tonight. In the house, probably.

"Eddie'll be real pleased, Tom," Dan said as he took the bridle. "You should come over."

"I've been trying to get the time," Tom said as he turned away from Dan and went back to the men beside the wagons.

Dan examined his grain with appraising eyes next morning. The heads looked long and firm and they were well filled with kernels. But how long should the head be to average eighteen to twenty bushels to the acre? How many kernels to a stalk? How many stalks . . . Dan wondered if Pa or Mom knew. They must be figuring too.

The threshers left the neighborhood before either Dan or the Nelsons had finished shocking their grain. Across the fields Jim Jackson started off, taking his first load to Minot. How much had his land actually yielded, Dan wondered. Less than fifteen bushels to the acre, he was certain. How was it going to grade?

Squatter Smith came again the last day of harvest and worked in the field with Mom and Dan.

"I brought a couple of rabbits," he told Mom as he helped stack the shocks. "I figured you folks hadn't time to catch much meat, and Osborne said I was right. He'll likely have a good dish for us tonight. Can he cook, Red?"

"He can," Mom spoke up. "Our garden's at its prime now.

New potatoes, carrots, onions, everything. Only thing we can't raise out here is fruit, I guess."

"Can't be sure of any top-of-the-ground stuff except grain," Squatter told her. "If you don't start covering those squash and things you won't have any. Frost can come any night after the end of August."

"That's what the literature said," Mom agreed. "So we've got enough root vegetables to feed an army."

"You'll need them before another harvest rolls around," Squatter warned. "And all the meat you can salt down, too. Pheasants and rabbits are all right when you can space them with a little pork and beef. They get tiresome, otherwise."

"We can get pork from the Nelsons," Mom assured him. "And we've got calves ready for slaughter. Raising pigs was just more than we could undertake this first year. I can cull out the chickens during the winter. We'll get by for food all right."

Dan watched her as she said it. She knew. Yes, Mom knew just how they were going to come out with the income from the crops.

But it was hard to realize that things were bad when they gathered around the table that night. Pa and Grace had made baking powder biscuits and the rabbit stew was topped with golden mounds. They'd made a cake too, and put raisins in the frosting.

Sugar, Dan thought. Flour and baking powder and salt and coffee. Kerosene oil and coal. Those were things the farm would not produce. They had to be bought in Minot. And shoes. How much would $250 or $300 buy?

A knock at the kitchen door ended his speculations. Mom called "Come in" but before the words were out, Jim Jackson was there staring at them and the look on his face was frightening.

"Jim," everyone said at once. "What's the matter?"

Mom got a chair for him and drew it to the table. She cut a piece of cake, but good as it looked he shook his head.

"I'll take it home to Ida, if you don't mind," he said and his voice didn't sound like Jim.

"There's plenty for you both," Mom said. "Have you had any supper? Grace, get a clean plate."

He eyed the supper table, then looked away.

"I don't feel right . . . without Ida."

"We'll send a plate home to her," Mom assured him. "Now, Jim, tell us what's the matter. Ida isn't sick, is she? Maybe we can help."

"You can't help. Nobody can help."

He sat down, elbows on the table, and hid his face in his hands.

"I'm ruint."

"You're too young to be ruined," Pa spoke up, "No matter what's happened."

"What's the matter, Jim," Dan urged but as he asked the question he thought he knew. "Don't mind Squatter being here. He's like one of the family. He knows all about farmers' problems."

Jim looked across the table at Squatter, then back at the plate of food Mom was pushing toward him and his hand reached for a fork.

"I'm washed up, that's all," he said. "The Interests have cleaned me out!"

Dan looked away from Mom. He couldn't face her. He got up and put the coffee pot back on the stove to heat.

"You know how much I can get for all my grain this year?"

he heard Jim saying. "Four hundred dollars. And I owe $800 and the 12% interest to boot."

It was like a torrent, once he started talking.

"You know how much my yield was? Twelve bushel to the acre and I only got seventy acres in. When I got it to the elevator in Minot they graded it No. 4 but it was good No. 1 wheat. The threshers said so. But the elevator graded it No. 4. Said it was shriveled and had too much cockle. They took off three pounds for dockage and there wasn't that much dirt in it. Their scales weighed it less than the true weight, too. I know it."

"Why didn't you take it to the county scales first?" Squatter asked.

"County scales? I didn't know there wuz any county scales. That little wouldn't have made no real difference anyhow. They'd only pay 60¢ for No. 4 wheat. And I owe over $800. It'll take $100 for seed for next spring if I could get 100 acres in, which is about all one man can do alone. You gotta figger a dollar an acre for seed."

Mom nodded.

"So that leaves me $300 to pay off the debt and live another year, so you can see." His voice was bitter.

"What did they say at the Loan Office?" Mom asked.

"They'll take all the cash I kin get fer the grain and write out a new loan. Charge me another extry $50 fer fixin' it up. So I'll be owin' almost as much as a year ago, and without a cent to live on. Oh, they're scoundrels! Dirty, blood-suckin' scoundrels!"

No one knew what to say. Jim's bitterness was frightening.

"I figgered it out on the way home. I couldn't get outa debt by the time I prove up, even if we had good crops every year.

A new house? We'd never get out of that sod shanty. I'll never get out of debt."

"Jim," Pa said kindly. "It couldn't be that bad."

"Sure it is!" Jim insisted. "Figger it out yourself."

Item by item, Jim had figured it out. What he could hope to get for his grain. What it would cost to live.

"No, Osborne, it's no use," he insisted. "I'm ruint."

"I thought . . ." Dan hesitated to say it but he did. "I thought Ike Sheets had influence, Jim. Can't he get the loan fixed up for you without that extra $50 charge every time?"

"Ike Sheets!" Jim snorted. "Influence! That's what he said. He's just another scoundrel, waiting to see what he kin git out of it, once I pull out. He knows I've got to go. He's just waitin' like a vulture."

"Pull out?" Mom asked. "What are you going to do, Jim?"

"Take Ida home to her folks in Nebrasky, Missus Osborne," Jim said. "You don't know it but she's . . . well, we're going to have a baby. She can't stay here an' starve no longer. We ain't hardly had a decent meal in months."

"Well, you eat this one before it gets any colder," Mom said pouring the hot coffee Dan brought from the stove. "I'm going right over to Ida tonight."

"She'll appreciate the sight of a woman," Jim said as he began his supper at last.

There wasn't anything anyone could say. Dan knew that Mom was rebuking herself for not having gone to see Ida before. Mentally he again tried to figure how the Osbornes would come out, after paying up the $250 loan. There mustn't be any more borrowing. Not after Jim's experience. The little money they had left this year would have to stretch for coal and kerosene oil and things they couldn't do without.

"Here's what I come over for tonight," Jim said as he

settled back after finishing his cake. "I turned over all the money I got for the grain yesterday. There's enough grain left to pay something on two of the horses. The other two and the tools that ain't paid for, I'll leave. If you folks could give me $50 for the plow and seeder and harrow, I'd have enough to pack Ida up and get out, takin' only what we brought with us. Why should I haul the grain to Minot? Let 'em come and git it!"

"Would it be honest?" Pa asked.

"More honest than they've been with me," Jim replied bitterly. "The tools I'm offerin' to sell you is all paid fer and I've got the receipts. 'Nother thing, if I don't sell 'em to you, or mebee the Nelsons, Ike Sheets'll steal 'em, soon as he knows I'm gone. I figger you can use more farmin' tools, an' the Nelsons have got all they need."

"Fifty dollars isn't enough for the plow and seeder and harrow," Mom said reluctantly. Dan knew what she was thinking. With those tools they both could work on the land at once, this fall and again in the spring.

"It's more'n they'll allow me for 'em, second handed," Jim said. "I tried to figger out if I sold everythin', could I pay off the debt and still have $50 to get out with. I couldn't. They don't allow you nothin' fer the stuff they charged you top prices for, if you have to turn it in. They jest take it. They'll take the harvester. They'll be out here after everything by day-after-tomorrow, if I'm not back with the second load of grain."

"You think they've an idea of what you're planning to do?" Pa asked and his face was serious in the lamp light.

"I didn't tell 'em but I ain't the first one they've cleaned out," Jim replied. "My head was poundin' so when I left the Loan Office I hardly know what I said. They wouldn't even allow me $5 for groceries. Said they'd fix it up so I'd have money for eatin' when I brought in the next load of grain. But I ain't goin' to haul more grain for 'em. Not if you folks can help me out."

Dan looked at Mom. It was a chance to get the farming tools they needed at a good price and help Jim, too. If they didn't he'd have to haul the rest of his grain to Minot and turn over everything to the Loan Office.

"Sure you've got clear title to the tools, Jim?" Squatter asked, entering the conversation for the first time.

"I bought 'em outright and paid for 'em with the first money I borrowed," Jim said. "I'll give Osborne all the papers. I wouldn't do nothin' underhanded."

Leaving the Loan Office to collect as best it could did not seem wrong to Jim. But Squatter didn't see it that way.

"You say this Ike Sheets will steal everything as soon as you're gone," he said. "How do you know the Loan Office will get the grain and tools and horses you're leaving for them if he'll steal everything?"

"That's their lookout," he muttered. "What I need now is $50 to get Ida some decent food and get her home."

Pa looked at Mom. It was plain that they both were nervous.

"Jim, I think Pa and I both want to help you all we can. And we need the tools, too. But to tell you the truth, we haven't got $50. Not until we sell our grain."

The only sound in the room was Jim's heavy breathing. It was a gasping sound and he sunk his head in his hands again. Mom walked over to the big chest and came back with the old black purse, which she gave to Pa.

"Jim, we've got just about $35," Pa said. "It's not enough for your tools. Maybe it'll pay for the plow and harrow, second hand."

Jim lifted his head then and the look of relief on his face made Dan choke and turn away.

"We kin get by with that," he whispered. "I'll make out a bill of sale for all the stuff, anyway. It'll be stole or taken in on the debt, if you don't get it. Dan can help me bring it over tomorrow night, then Ida and me'll start back to Nebrasky."

"The only way we'll take it all is to owe you the balance, Jim," Pa said. "You can let us know where to send the $15."

Jim nodded. "That'll be fine," he said. "It'll be something for Ida to have while I'm lookin' for work. There's one thing I want to warn you about though," he added as though it came to him suddenly. "The threshin' crew that did my grain told me one of them outfits workin' out from Williston ain't to be trusted. They've been stealin' grain most every place they thresh. I most forgot to tell you, what with all my own worries."

"Which outfit?" Pa and Dan asked at the same time. "How're they stealing it?"

"I don't rightly know them things," Jim said. "I should of asked more questions."

Squatter got up from the table and limped over to the water pail for a drink. When he came back he had a worn black purse in his hand.

"If the Osbornes would just as soon, they can owe me instead of you," Squatter said. "I'll make up the $15 so you can have it all now."

Everyone was looking at Squatter then, thin and bent over but smiling a little when he brought out the money.

"You'd better make out a bill of sale so I can witness it and make certain it's legal," he said so Dan brought paper and ink while Mom packed a basket of food and prepared to go home with Jim.

"No need for you to come now," Jim said. "She ain't sick, but I'm skeered she'll take a fit of cryin' when I tell her everything. Especially if you bring food and all."

"I'll come tomorrow then," Mom promised.

No one spoke for a time after Jim had gone. Dan knew what Pa and Mom were thinking. They'd got a bargain on the tools, but how were they going to fare when Dan took their grain to the elevator.

"I wonder if a fellow would do better to take his grain somewhere beside Minot," Dan finally asked.

"No," Squatter said at once. "The elevators all belong to the same chain. They all grade the same way and pay the same price, all over North Dakota. But weigh it at the county scales before you go to the elevator."

"Gosh, Squatter, what can a fellow do?" Dan groaned. "They grade your grain any way they want to and that's the lowest grade. They weigh it short and take off too much for dockage and pay you the lowest price. How are the farmers ever going to get Jim Hill and the Interests out of North Dakota?"

"That's not what's needed. You know that," Squatter said and there was reproach in his voice. "If Jim Hill took everything out of North Dakota that he's put into it, where would you be? Jim Hill's blamed for all the crooked dealings of all the unscrupulous people who followed his railroad into the state."

No one answered Squatter and after a little he started talking again.

"Take this boy, Jim Jackson," he said. "Do you suppose Jim Hill or anyone in Minneapolis is to blame for his failure?"

"The Loan Office is," Dan insisted. "They get their money

from the bank, don't they? And the banks get their money from Minneapolis."

"The mistake was in loaning him the money in the first place," Squatter said. "Of course 12% interest is too high. And $50 for fixing up the loan is crooked. There's a bankers' association in this state now and in time they'll put a stop to such things. But in the meantime, see what's happening to the Loan Office."

Dan couldn't answer him. Jim Jackson wasn't going to pay the Loan Office.

"It takes time to get the right men to Bismarck and the right laws passed," Squatter went on. "A chap with only $50 to his name shouldn't be allowed to go into debt for more than he can possibly pay off. It takes more than $50 capital to start a 160-acre farm."

"We had close to $3,000 and we've sunk it all in this homestead," Mom spoke up. "Right now it seems as though even that wasn't enough."

14. The Stewart Family

"DAN, there's something I've got to ask you. What about your brother Slim?"

Dan almost dropped the cookies Squatter had brought out to the plow for him. They were sitting on the ground beside the freshly turned furrows eating the lunch Mom had fixed when Squatter asked the question.

Dan stopped eating. "What do you mean?" he asked.

Squatter wiped his fingers on the grass.

"I mean I've got to know," he said without looking at Dan. "Everything. Your Pa can be elected county school commissioner unless there's something . . . well, I guess you know what I mean."

Dan didn't answer.

"I've been sounding out the men over East," Squatter went on. "They're all McKinley and Roosevelt men. They'll vote the Republican ticket like they intended, if they can be sure of your Pa. But skeletons don't stay in family closets in an election fight, Red."

Dan felt his cheeks growing hot.

"Has anyone said anything against Slim?" he asked. Who could Squatter have been talking to?

"No one but you folks yourselves," Squatter told him. "Whenever his name is mentioned . . . well, you know."

Dan knew. Whenever Slim's name was mentioned they talked about something else. More than once, Dan now recalled, Squatter had spoken of Slim. Yes, he and Mom and Pa were the ones who had raised a doubt in Squatter's mind.

"Squatter, I don't know what to say," Dan finally told him. "Slim's in trouble somehow but we don't know what it is."

"Then you've got to find out."

"We can't," Dan protested. "We don't know how. He came home but he didn't tell us anything and he left without even saying goodbye."

"Do you know where he is?"

"In Williston."

"Then you'd better go to Williston and ask him right out," Squatter advised. "Tell him about Anderson. Tell him your father can be elected this fall. Can go on to the legislature two years from now if his health continues to improve . . . unless there's something the opposition finds out and can use to hang him with."

"The legislature?" Dan almost gasped. "But Pa said . . ."

Squatter's penetrating eyes were on Dan again.

"I know what he said. But the people would have something to say, too. He's the kind of man they'd support. The man they're looking for and want to send to Bismarck."

Dan folded his arms across his knees and stared at his empty furrows. He'd never been to Bismarck, but he could see Pa there . . . dressed in his store clothes . . . leaning on a cane perhaps, but all the more dignified because of it. Yes, the men in North Dakota would listen to Pa, if he could just get started. Just get elected this fall.

But to go to Williston again! Face Slim and ask embarrassing questions. How was he to get away without telling Mom and Pa? Dan felt his shoulders sagging. He hadn't been prepared for this new demand.

"What am I going to say to the folks?" he asked. "I can't just take off with no reason at all."

"You ought to be lining up a threshing outfit," Squatter suggested.

So once more Dan rode into Williston looking for Slim. He knew Mom and Pa had questioned his reason for going, but they hadn't said much.

The streets of the town were thick with mid-summer dust and the buildings squatted like baked potatoes, brown-drab in the sun. A few children stared, a few dogs yapped while Dan rode to the restaurant where he had first found Slim. The place was empty and the waiter was sitting against the wall, his long legs stretched out into the room. He jumped to his feet as Dan closed the door noisily.

"Is Slim around?" Dan asked.

The man stared at him for a few seconds before answering. "You're the feller who wuz here to see him last spring, ain't you?"

"Yes."

"Well, he ain't here."

"Where is he?"

"What ye want to know fer?"

"Look, I'm his brother," Dan said. "This is family business."

The man squinted his eyes and peered at Dan. "Not much family resemblance," he observed. Then, "Slim ain't in Williston right now."

Dan knew that his mouth dropped open at the news.

"The boss has him out with one of the threshin' crews," the waiter went on.

Dan sank into a chair and ran his hands through his hair. He'd have to follow Slim.

"Do you know where the threshing crew is?" he asked.

"One crew went up north an' wuz to swing off east an' back. T'other wuz to go southwest, then east an' back. But I don't know which crew he's with, an' that's a fact."

Dan believed him. He wondered whether the waiter knew anything about Slim's life or his job or his connection with the Interests, but he couldn't bring himself to ask this man about his brother. Someone must know, though. Mr. Parker, perhaps?

"Do you know a fellow named Isaiah Parker?" Dan asked.

"Never heered of him. Does he live in Williston?"

"Off southwest. Slim and I both know him. Maybe Slim's gone that way. Can you pack up a lunch box for me? Enough for a couple of days, while I try to locate him?"

"Sure thing."

Alone at the table, Dan let his mind wander back to Mr. Parker. He'd start southwest and if Slim wasn't with that crew he'd ride home by way of the coulee. Mr. Parker must know something. It was like prying into Slim's business behind his back, but Pa himself had first had the thought.

It was not difficult to follow the threshing crew for the farmers Dan questioned were eager to talk. Most of them were complaining and accusing.

"You ain't the sheriff, be ye?" one farmer asked. "If ever a passel of thieves got onto my land it wuz this threshin' outfit. 'T'ain't enough to charge more'n it's worth to thresh. They must-a stole 75 to 100 bushel of grain too."

"Stole?" The word sent a chill through Dan and he had heard it hinted more than once as he trailed the threshing crew. This time Slim was with a gang of thieves for sure, Dan thought. But he wasn't among the "hands" when Dan at last overtook the outfit.

"Osborne? Sure I know him," the crew boss said. "Been workin' in a restaurant in Williston, ain't he? He's in charge of the cook car with the other threshin' crew."

There was a grain of comfort in the news. If Slim was in charge of the cook car, perhaps he didn't even know there was stealing going on, Dan tried to tell himself. But when he thought of Slim that possibility faded. Slim would know what was going on!

Wearily Dan headed for the coulee. He dreaded seeing Mr. Parker. Dreaded questioning him. Slowly he rode the last miles. Here the horse thieves had hidden out; here the sheep had been trapped. Stately tiger lilies nodded in the sun where lambs had died. Goldenrod covered the hillside where he had slid and fallen in the darkness. It all reminded him of Slim.

There were no dogs in the Parker's yard today. When Dan called out, Mrs. Parker came to the doorway.

"Mr. Parker home?" Dan asked.

She shook her head. "He's off workin' with the threshin' crew."

Blankly Dan stared at her. It couldn't be! This long ride, first to Williston then back to the coulee, and for nothing. First Slim and then Mr. Parker gone!

"Mind if I water my horse?" Dan asked at last and turned Prince toward the well. Stiffly he dismounted and stood beside

Prince, resting his head against the black neck. He'd missed out altogether. Either he'd have to go back to Williston and follow the trail of the other crew or go home and tell Squatter he'd failed. And that would mean Pa couldn't win the election, for Squatter had as good as said he must know about Slim if he was going to help Pa.

So he'd go back to Williston!

He straightened his shoulders and lifted his head, and then he saw Mrs. Parker standing on the other side of the big wooden tub.

"What did you want to see my man about?" she asked.

Dan didn't answer. Just stared at the torn flounce on her faded blue wrapper.

"Wuz it the debt again?" she asked. "Did Slim send you?"

Dan shook his head.

"Pa and Slim is workin' with the same threshin' outfit. Likely you know. They otta get the debt squared away this fall and everythin' straightened out."

Dan stared at the thin, tired face scarce understanding what the woman was saying. Wisps of straight, graying hair were blowing across her eyes and she moved one hand over her forehead in a futile gesture. Her lips were trembling a little and the eyes that met Dan's were pleading. Suddenly Dan realized that Mrs. Parker knew the story, whatever it was. And she'd tell him!

"Mrs. Parker, Slim didn't send me," Dan explained. "Pa and I want to find him. We want to help him, but we don't know what's wrong or how to help."

For a moment she hesitated, then she began telling the cruel, bitter story . . .

"I keep hopin' that now they're workin' together again, it'll all come out right. It's hurt Pa and me for things to be

-195-

like this between him and Slim when once they wuz partners, and him almost like a son to us . . ."

She pushed the hair out of her eyes again.

"I don't trust the feller who owns these threshin' machines, but Pa and Slim ain't responsible fer what he does . . ."

Dan knew, as the woman talked, that he must get home and tell Squatter the whole truth, and then find Slim before it was too late—if it wasn't too late already.

"Faster, Prince, faster!"

Once more the long black legs reached out, pushing burned-over miles behind them. Dan must get home. He must find Slim. There was no time to lose.

It was late afternoon when the willows and the home buildings came into view. There they sat, and the stubble and the shocks of grain beyond them, and the sight set Dan's heart to beating faster. This was what the Osbornes had come to North Dakota for, and there it was. All they'd hoped for and more, at their very grasp. Pa about to be somebody. Not just a farmer. An agricultural statesman, that's what John Worst had said. An agricultural statesman in Bismarck, fighting to keep the wealth of North Dakota for the farmers who produced it. It was all theirs, if he could just stop Slim before it was too late!

Dan galloped right into the yard before he realized that something was wrong. No one had come to meet him. Not even Punkin with his welcoming yaps. He sat still for a minute as Prince panted and shook his head, edging toward the water trough. Then Dan saw Grace. She was sitting on the back steps hugging her poor rag doll, tears streaming down her face.

"Grace! What's the matter? Where's everybody?"

"Oh Dan," she sobbed. "Eddie's gone."

"Eddie's gone?" He just sat there and repeated the words. "Eddie's gone? Where? What do you mean, Grace?"

Between sobs she told him, wiping her tears on the doll's torn dress.

"He must-a went this morning," she said. "He must-a gone hunting for Slim. When Mom called us at noon, he didn't come."

Dan's eyes turned to the horses.

"He didn't take a horse," Grace told him. "He didn't take nuthin'."

"If he'd gone looking for Slim he'd have taken a horse," Dan reasoned. "You're sure he isn't hiding somewhere? In the hay mow?"

"Mom and Squatter looked everywhere," Grace insisted. "I took Punkin out in the field and called and called."

Dan knew, without asking, that everyone was out looking for Eddie. Even Pa, for the wagon was gone.

"Which way did they go?" he asked.

"Pa and Mom started off Williston way," Grace said. "Squatter went for the Nelson boys and they've gone off east and south. A little while ago Squatter came circling back north. He's hunting in the wheat shocks again, but Eddie isn't there."

Dan looked across the field with its rows of golden bee-hives. He could see Squatter, riding slowly northward.

"Has anyone looked around Jim Jackson's place?" Dan asked. "Maybe he climbed on the sod roof of Jim's barn and fell through."

"Maybe he did, Dan," she said and a gleam of hope light-ened her tragic face. "Nobody thought of that. You go look. Mom told me to sit right here and not go no place."

Prince wanted a drink all right, but he could wait. Eddie had to be somewhere within a radius of ten miles, certainly. His little legs wouldn't carry him much more than a couple of miles an hour. If he'd planned to go far, like to Williston to look for Slim, he'd have taken a horse. More likely he'd just gone off by himself, to dream or hunt for more of the colored clay pebbles Tom had found, Dan tried to assure himself. But by now he should have been hungry and come home.

Dan scanned every clump of thistles and every rose cluster as he hurried toward Jim Jackson's abandoned sod buildings. Tumbleweeds swirled past him in the wind and every bouncing ball gave him a start. Ahead the prairie lay flat and unobstructed except for one rolling hill off at the northwest section of the Osborne farm, and Squatter was riding in that direction. If Eddie was playing in the slough beyond the hill, Squatter would find him.

The more Dan thought about it, the less likely it seemed that Eddie could be trapped in Jim's old buildings. He could have called and surely Tom would have heard him, for the Sheets' shanty was just across the road. Maybe he'd climbed onto Jim's straw stack and it had caved in on him. The thought was terrifying.

"Come on, Prince!"

But just as Dan started the horse galloping, a frightened cry came to him from a distance.

"Pa! . . . Help!"

It was Eddie. Dan knew it before he could sense where the sound came from; before he could see anything except a blur of gray prairie and black sod buildings.

"Pa! . . . Pa!"

He swung Prince sharply and started, his eyes searching the prairie. Another minute and Eddie was climbing over the top of the hill, scrambling, falling, getting up and running again.

Dan heard Squatter shouting, and the next instant Ike Sheets appeared, climbing over the top of the hill and racing after Eddie. He was carrying a heavy spade and as he ran Dan saw him swing it up over his shoulder.

"Eddie!" Dan screamed.

Was Ike going to strike Eddie with that spade? He'd kill the boy. Was he mad altogether? He had beaten Tom, Dan was sure.

"Ike! Stop it!"

Prince was galloping now but Eddie could be dead before Dan got there if Ike really meant to strike. Dan watched in horror as the spade rose into the air. Then it shot skyward and fell to the ground and at the same instant Ike was careening crazily, spinning until he fell.

Squatter Smith, sling shot in hand, was off his horse and walking deliberately toward Ike, while Eddie raced to safety, arms outstretched toward Squatter, whose sling shot had saved him.

Dan didn't try to reason it out. His temples throbbed and his throat was dry as he hurried to his brother, burning with fury. Over the top of the hill Tom appeared, and when he saw his father on the ground he went to him slowly.

Ike had raised himself on one elbow by the time Dan got there. He was moaning and his right arm hung limp. Beside him Tom stood, white-faced and choking back his sobs.

"Uncle John," Tom begged. "Don't send him to jail. Please don't send him to jail."

Over the hulking, lubberly man stood Squatter Smith, gripping the sling shot in his hand.

"You'd even beat a child!" he said and his voice sounded

thick with hatred. "Don't you know you might have killed him?"

In amazement Dan looked from Squatter to Tom . . . "Uncle John" . . . These two men knew each other. Could they be brothers? Tom was crying openly and Eddie, safe beside Squatter, was watching him, wide-eyed.

"What's the meaning of this?" Squatter demanded of the man on the ground. "Tell me or I'll . . ." and he raised the handle of the sling shot as though to strike.

"Uncle John!" Tom cried again. "Don't . . . Please don't."

Squatter let the sling shot drop limp in his hand.

"Tom, tell me what happened," he demanded.

But Tom only looked at his father and wiped his tear-streaked face on the sleeve of his ragged shirt.

Dan dismounted and went to Eddie. On his knees, arms around the boy, he got the story.

"Ike said it's a tunnel leading right down to Hell," Eddie said. "It's a big, black hole right under the hill. He said I mustn't tell or he'd throw me down there. But I didn't believe him. I said I was going to tell Pa."

Squatter turned quickly to Eddie.

"A big black hole? Black all around on the ground too?" he asked. Then before Eddie could answer, Squatter turned to Ike again.

"Lignite?" he asked. "Lignite, and on the Osborne land? Is that it?"

Ike looked away and didn't answer, but Squatter's mind apparently had raced ahead and he didn't need an answer.

"You were stealing it when the kid caught you in the act! Oh, I know you! Get up!"

Ike didn't try to get up. He moved one shoulder a little and groaned.

"What're you going to do?" he asked. It was the first time he had spoken.

"It's not what I'm going to do this time. It's what Osborne's going to do. I hope he sends you to jail. That's what I should have done five years ago. Get up!"

Tom helped his father to his feet.

"How much have you taken?" Squatter demanded and when Ike didn't answer he turned to Tom again.

"How long has he been taking it?"

Tom started to speak but as he opened his mouth Ike struck at him with his good hand, and Tom darted back. Then Squatter lunged at Ike and for all the difference in their size, he knocked the huge man to the ground again.

"You're not going to touch Tom," Squatter fairly snarled. "You're never going to strike him again. If Osborne doesn't send you to jail, I will. To think that I've been hiding out like a rat on this prairie for five years because of you!"

He turned to Dan at last. "Is this the man you call Ike Sheets?" he asked.

"Yes."

"Well, his name is Frank Stewart, and he's my half-brother," Squatter said. "And my name isn't Squatter Smith. It's John Stewart."

He held his head proudly and he said it defiantly. Then he turned back to Ike.

"Why did you have to do this?" he demanded. "If there's lignite here, it's under your land too, likely enough. But it was easier to get at here. You'd rather steal it than hunt for it on your own land. Why have you always had to be like this?"

Ike didn't answer.

"You had just as good a job with Jim Hill as I had," Squatter went on. "But because I worked in the office and you in the yard, you felt I had more than you. You were jealous and resentful. That was all, wasn't it?"

Squatter stuck the sling shot back in his belt.

"That was your fault too," he went on. "You had the same chance as I, and you were smart enough. Smart enough to take my pass key night after night and go back to the yard and steal!"

He said the words bitterly, and both Ike and Tom avoided his eyes.

"Don't think I'll ever go back to Minneapolis and pay for the stuff you took. Then they would think I was the one who took it. There'll be suspicion on me the rest of my life, because of you!"

Dan drew Eddie closer to him and looked away. It was clear now why Squatter Smith had never filed on his land, even though he could have done it. Clear why he'd been suspicious the day Dan stumbled into his valley. Why he'd been reluctant to help Pa openly in the election campaign. He'd been living in fear ever since he'd left Minneapolis to squat on a claim out on the prairie.

It was Eddie who finally spoke.

"He was mean to Tom, Squatter," Eddie said. "Tom wanted him to let me go home, but he said I couldn't go until I promised not to tell. He said I'd have to stay in the hole all night. For a month, maybe. He said he could set fire to the hole after he'd put me in it, and it would burn all the way under our land and burn up the world!"

Eddie's voice was tense and he shrilled out the story. Squatter smiled a little and looked from Eddie to Tom.

"Come here, Tom," he said. "I'm going to take you back to the Osbornes' with me."

Tom looked away from all of them and stared at the ground. "The Osbornes don't want me," he said.

Dan got up then. "Don't say that, Tom. We'll let by-gones be by-gones."

"What do you mean?" Squatter demanded quickly, looking first at Dan and then at his nephew.

"I done things," Tom said, kicking at a tuft of grass. "I slung a rock at his horse once, with my sling shot. He knows I done it. He had everythin' an' I had nuthin'. He got the dog. He had folks," and he gestured toward Eddie without looking at him.

"So you let a rock fly at his horse," Squatter nodded understandingly.

"I didn't intend for Prince to break his hobbles and run away, though," Tom said earnestly, turning to look straight at Dan. "Honest, I didn't. I just . . . let her fly!"

So at last Dan knew what had happened. "Look, Tom, it's all right," he said. "Now that I know you didn't mean for Prince to get away, it's all right." Then he turned from Tom to Squatter. "Tom's done a lot of good things since then."

"What else that wasn't good?" Squatter asked. "Let's get it all wiped off the boards."

"I . . ." Tom hesitated, and moved a little farther away from his father. "I could-a found a way to let you know why we measured off your land. 'Specially when you didn't understand from the colored clay. I found it here. I thought you'd hunt for more, maybe."

Measuring off the land was something that Squatter hadn't known about, and Dan had to tell him.

"That wasn't Tom's fault," Dan insisted. "He had to help his old man. Only how did Ike figure out that our house was across the line on the Nelsons' land? That's what I'd like to know."

"He didn't know until we'd measured," Tom said. "It was the lignite we wuz measurin' for. It's almost on our land. We wuz measurin' to be sure it wasn't on our place. Just a couple of feet more an' it would-a been on our claim, not yours."

Squatter shook his head at this new evidence of his half-brother's dishonesty. Then he walked to Tom and put his arm around the boy's shoulders.

"You're going to live with me from now on, Tom," he said. "You're going to live right and have friends. And as for you, 'Ike Sheets' . . ."

He glared at Tom's father and there was no mistaking his meaning.

"The best thing for you to do is take that broken shoulder to a doctor in Minot, and if Osborne doesn't put the law on you, just keep on going!"

He held Tom closer to him. "Come on, we'll take Eddie home now," he said.

Without looking at his father Tom started with Squatter toward Dan and Eddie. He stopped suddenly as he neared them and lifted his head slightly.

"I hear wagons rollin'," he said.

Dan heard them too, and looking off to the northwest he saw the long line of hay racks etched against the sky, the threshing machine bringing up the rear.

"Oh, Squatter," Dan groaned. "It's one of those outfits from Williston. It's the crew that went north and they're swinging down this way. Slim's with them, and if they're like the crew that went south . . ."

It was hard to tell Squatter the story Mrs. Parker had told Dan, but he had to know it now.

"Get to Slim somehow and let him know what's at stake," Squatter said in a hushed voice as he and Dan, Tom and Eddie hurried back to the Osborne house. "Tom, you go line up the Nelsons to help with the threshing. You may as well tell them everything. If Slim's been in charge of the cook car, he could be in the clear. But he should quit the outfit now for your Pa's sake."

"What are you going to do?" Dan asked.

"I'm going back East and do some electioneering," Squatter said. "Electioneering I should have done long ago."

15. *Let the Wind Blow*

GETTING to Slim wasn't easy. Shorty Andrews, the thresh-ing crew boss, didn't let Slim out of his sight. With a loud-voiced show at friendliness he stayed with the Osborne men all evening. His crew, however, showed no friendliness. A sullen gang they appeared, talking to each other in under-tones and gathering in little groups of two or three. There was no cheerful camp fire, no singing, and they went to the bunk car early.

"You can stay here and sleep in your own room, can't you, Slim?" Mom asked when Shorty indicated it was time to "turn in." Slim looked at him questioningly.

"You know your own business," Shorty answered abruptly and left them.

Alone at last, no one seemed to know what to say. Pa, his voice hushed, finally asked Slim if everything was all right. "We've heard stories, Slim," he said.

Slim didn't look at Pa. They were in the living room, Slim with his legs stretched out as he half-sat, half-lay on Mom's sofa.

"Stories like what?" he asked.

"Dan went to Williston," Pa told him. "He followed the other crew south, trying to find you. It seems that outfit has a bad reputation."

"Why were you looking for me this time, Red?" Slim asked, ignoring Pa's remark.

"Because we needed you," Dan replied. "Pa can be elected county school commissioner this fall, and he'll be sent on to the legislature in Bismarck two years from now, if we can get a little electioneering done in the other end of the county this month . . . and if there aren't any skeletons in our family closet to prevent it."

Dan knew he had said it bluntly, but he hadn't meant to hurt Pa and Mom. They were both protesting his words at once. Ready to excuse Slim, no matter what he had done.

Slim's shoulders slumped at Dan's challenge. Finally he got up and walked to the window where he could look out at the row of grain wagons and racks and the threshing machine all lined up across the barn yard, and his cook car and the bunk car half-hidden by the thresher. When he spoke, his voice was hoarse and scarcely more than a whisper.

"What you heard about the outfit that went south holds for this one too," he said. "I told Shorty I didn't want anything taken from you, Pa, but he's boss. I'm not."

"Slim, if this is true why do you stay with the outfit?" Pa asked. His voice trembled but he went on, earnestly. "Surely there's some other job . . . some other outfit. You've had no part in the stealing. We never thought that. Only why do you stay?"

—207—

Hard-faced, but appealing too, Slim faced his father.

"You may as well know the whole story, Pa, if you don't know it already," he said. "I went into that sheep deal with Isaiah Parker as his partner. I wasn't old enough to file on a claim, but he could get one. The sheep were as much my idea as his. I put all my money into them and my name is on the notes, and we both owe the Loan Office. Now they're hounding the life out of us. Take every cent I earn before I ever get my hands on it. The restaurant, this threshing outfit, the Loan Office—they're all linked together because one way or another they all get their money back in Minneapolis. If I left the outfit now, I might not get paid even for the work I've put in. We don't get paid at all until the end of the season when we get back to Williston. Then what Parker and I get will be turned over on the debt. We figure that we can settle up, and maybe a few dollars to the good, if we finish the run."

Dan watched Pa's face as Slim talked. This was the story Mrs. Parker had told. It was the story Dan had repeated to Squatter Smith, but he'd had no chance to tell it all to Pa.

"Isaiah Parker's in the same fix, then," Pa said, and he sounded as beaten as Slim.

"Worse," Slim told him. "They'll take all he can make off his land next year if he doesn't work off what he owes now, like he agreed. Me, I've got nothing they can take but my horse. All I can do is work it out or light out . . . leaving a bad debt behind."

Slim's involvement with the Interests was perfectly clear to Pa and Mom now. The slow, morbid ticking of the clock was the only sound in the room.

"I told Shorty to let you alone," Slim said miserably. "There's only two in the crew that're in with him, and even those two are with me on this deal. But I don't know."

Dan spoke up then. "Slim, they're not going to steal the crops we slaved to raise!" he warned. "I'm going to stay in that granary all night tomorrow night. I'm going to take Punkin and my gun with me. You can tell Shorty Andrews that."

"I'll tell him," Slim said grimly. "He's going to accuse me of warning you, anyway. Now I might as well go back to the bunk car."

No one spoke as he walked out of the house. Slim wasn't going to stay with the family and sleep in his own bed as Mom had suggested. He wasn't going to leave the threshing outfit. His own involvement came first, ahead of Pa's chance to win the election, and Dan's cheeks burned at the thought.

It was a bitter Dan who hauled shocks of grain from the field to the threshing machine next day. If Shorty Andrews tried to steal any of it, there would be trouble that night. Dan told the Nelson boys and Tom to keep an eye on Shorty all day, for nobody knew when or how he would try to get the grain. Pa, meantime, was alert and watching in the barnyard. No one saw a suspicious move. In the evening, as soon as the men left the yard for the bunk car, Dan took his gun and blankets and with Punkin at his heels went to the granary where the mound of golden kernels was stored.

Dan scarcely dozed all night. He listened for every sound, and at the creak of a floor board he was awake. Punkin, restless too, was alert every time Dan wakened. Nobody tried the granary door, however. Apparently no one came near the building through the long, dark hours of night. Dan didn't care who saw him leave in the morning. He didn't care if Shorty thought Slim had passed on a warning.

Dan's feeling of satisfaction turned to bitterness and chagrin the next evening after the threshing crew drove out of the yard, however. With a silent gesture Pa led him and Tom and the Nelson boys to the side of the granary farthest from the house. Shoving straw and chaff from the side of the building he pointed to a loosened floor board, and the precious grain seeping down from the bins to the earth below. Speechlessly Dan stared until its full significance came to him. Sometime in the night, perhaps while he was on guard inside, or before he went into the granary, Shorty Andrews had worked from the outside and managed to steal their wheat.

"I'm showing Chris and Nels so they can warn their father," was all Pa said.

Dan groaned in despair. "Shorty's grain wagons were out in plain sight all the time. If he took more than a bushel or two, you'd have noticed it when you gave him his pay in grain. How could he get it off our farm without you knowing?"

Even as he asked, he knew the answer. The bunk car and the cook car had been close to the granary with the thresher between them and the house where Pa, too, had been watching all night, Dan was sure.

"Somewhere down the road I expect you could find them shifting bags of grain from the bunk car to Shorty's grain wagons," Pa said wearily. "Then they'll be all set to take their toll from the Nelsons, the same way."

"The bunk car," Dan repeated when his father left for the house. Tom and the Nelson boys were watching him, he knew. Probably they were thinking about the cook car, too.

"They're not a quarter of a mile away," Tom said. "They can't go fast. Seems like we could do something."

"There're some bad ruts in the trail," Nels suggested quietly. "I know about where."

The sun was sinking under darkening clouds when Dan and Tom, Chris and Nels, headed their horses across the prairie, paralleling the road. The wind was rising now. A gale would be all to the good, Dan thought. Like stealthy Indians they watched until they saw the first rig hit the rut, then like Indians they swooped down upon the swaying wagons, lashing at the team that hauled the bunk car. The horses lunged, the boys shouted, and the bunk car toppled on its side with an echoing crash. Jumping from his horse, Dan jerked the door open revealing hidden bags of grain. The next instant there was a shout from behind. It was Slim's voice calling to them to get out of the way, and on the wagon perch they saw him, knees bent, arms akimbo, driving his plunging cook car head on into the wreckage.

Slim was driving into the bunk car deliberately! Dan stared as pots and pans clanged across the prairie. Then Slim who had jumped just before the crash, pulled at the steps of the cook car and loosened a false bottom. More grain bags spilled out into the road.

Crew men began hurrying to the scene, but they were strangely silent. Shorty, who had been behind with the thresher, was last to arrive.

"You'll pay for this, Slim Osborne," he snarled.

"Tin dishes don't cost much," Slim told him. "What about this grain? It brings money."

"That's our grain and you all know it," Dan fairly shouted, but he realized when he spoke that the crew not only knew it but were taking sides. They were lining up behind Slim, and Mr. Parker was in the forefront with him. Their voices were angry and defiant.

"We've been waiting for a long time for this day," Mr. Parker said. "Slim and I figure we've worked out all we owe the Loan Office, and we go no farther unless there's a change made, here and now. The crew's with us, too. You can't go on without us!"

Shorty Andrews looked at his crew. Only two men were standing behind him.

"You'll answer for this in Williston," he warned.

"That's right. All of us together," Mr. Parker said. "Now I say the Osborne fellers should take their grain back home. Every man but two is willing to testify it's theirs."

Dan had not seen Mr. Nelson when he drove up, but he pushed his way to the front of the angry group of men. He towered like a giant over Shorty Andrews.

"I've heard of mutiny at sea," he said calmly. "I think you men have a right to do something like that here, and name a new crew boss. If you want to thresh my place tomorrow, it's got to be with Parker in charge."

"Parker!" There was assent in the voices that called out the name.

"All right," Mr. Nelson said. "Now how about helping him clear up this mess. I'll drive the Osbornes home with their grain."

They all talked at once on the way home. They even failed to notice three rigs tied to the hitching posts until Tom pointed to them.

"That's Uncle John's horse," Tom said.

"The election!" Dan exclaimed. "It has something to do with Pa's being elected."

They tied Mr. Nelson's team quickly. Heads bent against the rising gale they hurried to the house. The living-room was filled with men Dan did not know, and in front of them Squatter Smith stood, talking.

"I wanted you men to meet Osborne and hear what he has to say," Dan heard Squatter saying. "If you don't think he's a man of his word, don't vote for him. But I think he is, and that he's the kind of man this state needs in public office. The kind who'd dare oppose what you call the Interests. He has a reason to oppose them. And you, Anderson, I want you to know him before you go out campaigning against him."

Chairs scraped and there was a murmur of voices when Pa got up. His first words sent a chill through Dan.

"I'll not run for public office under any false colors," Pa said. "Nor with any subterfuge or anything held back from you . . ."

"Slim!" Dan gasped. "Pa doesn't know what's happened. He's going to tell . . ."

Slim didn't answer. He walked straight into the room and up to Pa, while Dan stood scarce daring to breathe. Pa's face twitched a little as he looked from Slim to the men around him. In the sudden quietness the sound of the barn door banging in the wind seemed to fill the room.

"This is my son," Pa said at last, so low Dan could hardly hear him.

"Let me tell it, Pa," Slim said and as Pa nodded Slim pulled out a chair and pushed it toward his father. Then he told his story, right up to the grain bags now safely in Mr. Nelson's wagon and in the yard outside.

Squatter Smith grasped Slim's hand when he finished, and Mr. Nelson shoved his way to the front of the room and clapped him on the shoulder. Then everybody began asking questions at once, and finally a big, blonde man made his way to Mr. Nelson's side and spoke to him in Norwegian. Then the man hammered on the table for attention.

"I want you all to know that Anderson's voting for Osborne," he shouted. "I'm Anderson."

Slim made his way to the door where Dan still was standing.

"Maybe the election'll come out all right," he said. "How does it look now, Red?"

"It looks like I can stop worrying about everything except the fall plowing," Dan replied. "And whether the wind's going to blow the barn away."

"If it does, there'll be two of us to haul it back," Slim said quietly.

"Then let her blow!" Dan said.